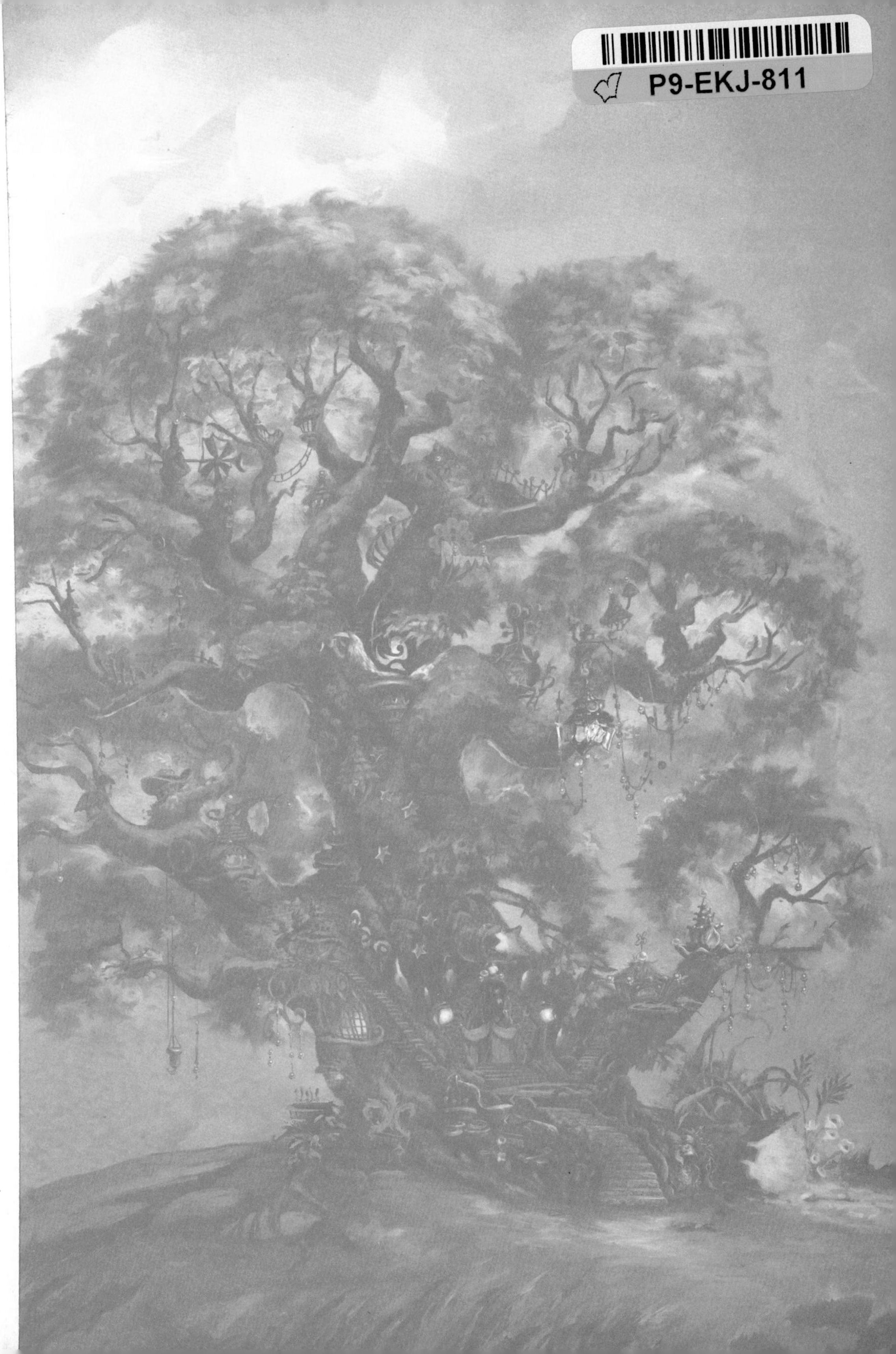

Disney Fairies

Tinker Bell

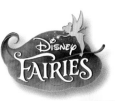

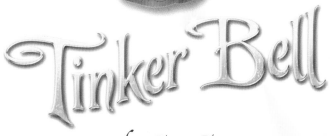

and a Far-Too-Secret Secret

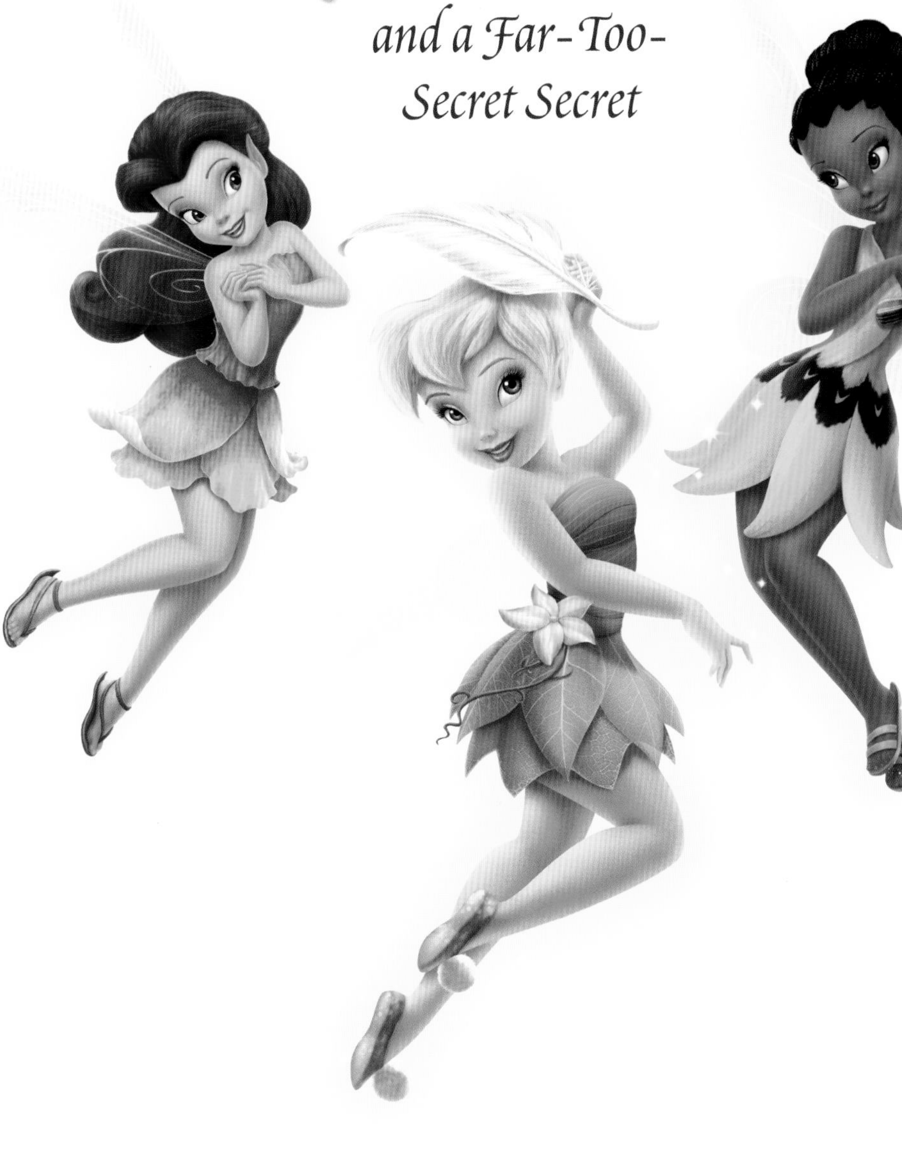

PAPERCUTZ™

Graphic Novels Available from PAPERCUTZ

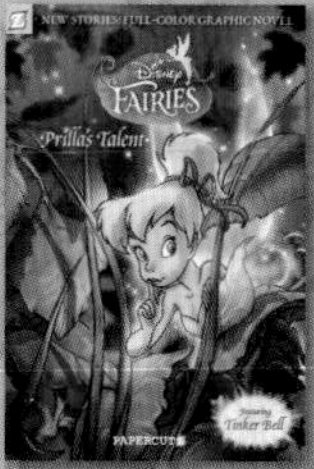

Graphic Novel #1
"Prilla's Talent"

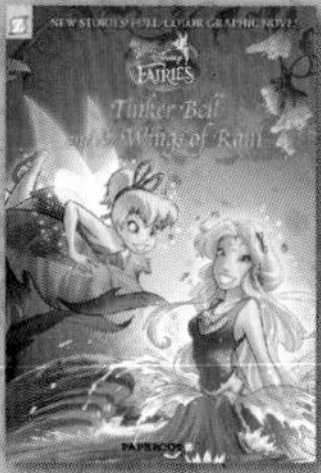

Graphic Novel #2
"Tinker Bell and the Wings of Rani"

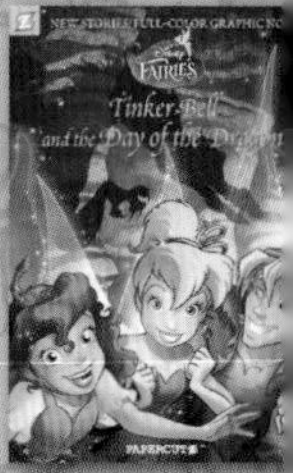

Graphic Novel #
"Tinker Bell and t Day of the Drago

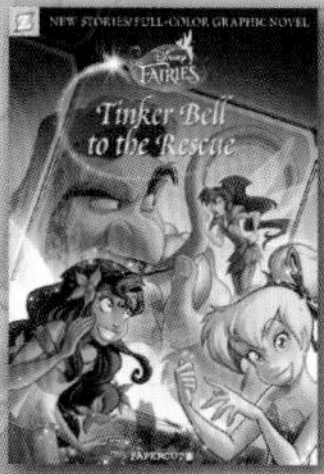

Graphic Novel #4
"Tinker Bell to the Rescue"

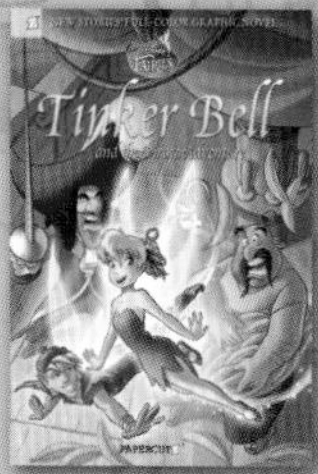

Graphic Novel #5
"Tinker Bell and the Pirate Adventure"

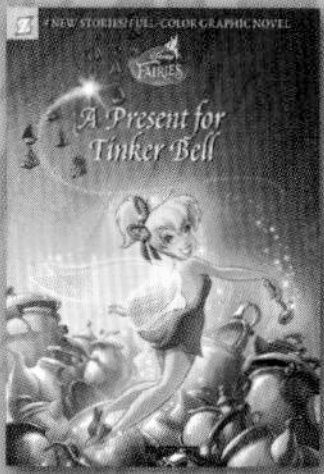

Graphic Novel #6
"A Present for Tinker Bell"

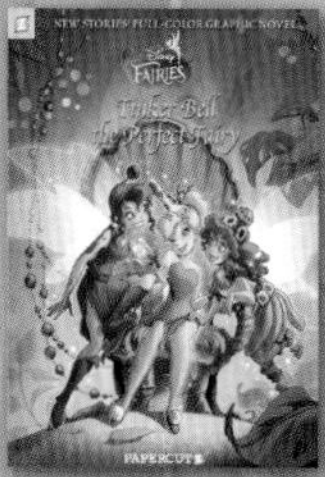

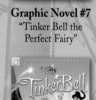

Graphic Novel #7
"Tinker Bell the Perfect Fairy"

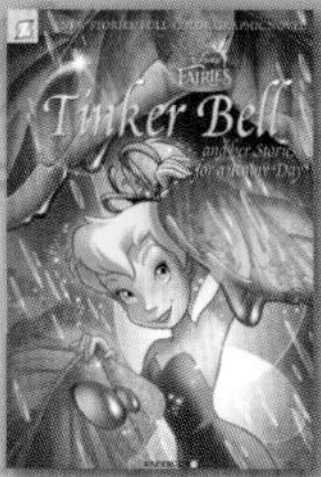

Graphic Novel #8
"Tinker Bell and her Stories for a Rainy Day"

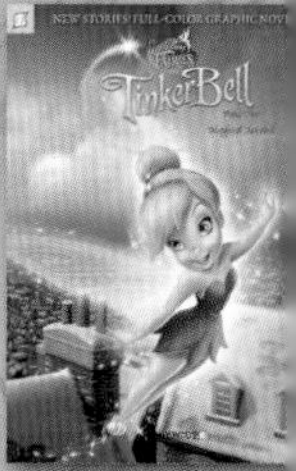

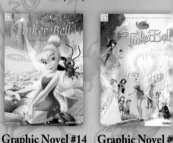

Graphic Novel #
"Tinker Bell and her Magical Arriv

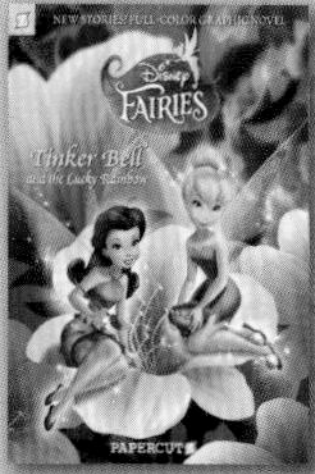

Graphic Novel #10
"Tinker Bell and the Lucky Rainbow"

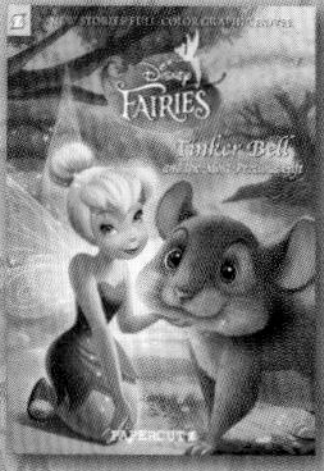

Graphic Novel #11
"Tinker Bell and the Most Precious Gift"

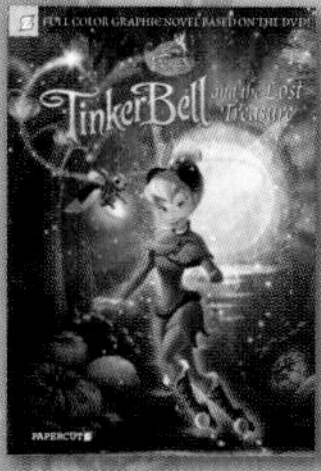

Graphic Novel #12
"Tinker Bell and the Lost Treasure"

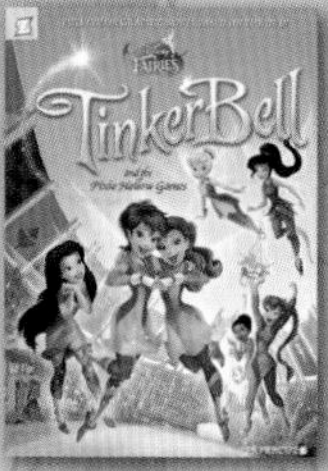

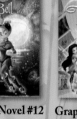

Graphic Novel #13
"Tinker Bell and the Pixie Hollow Games"

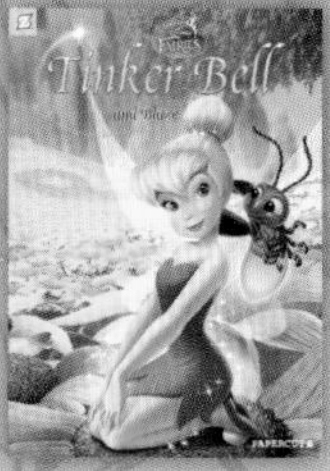

Graphic Novel #14
"Tinker Bell and Blaze"

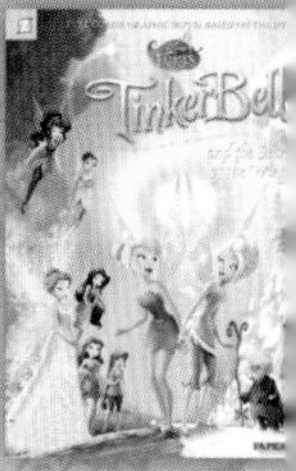

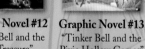

Graphic Novel #
"Tinker Bell and t Secret of the Win

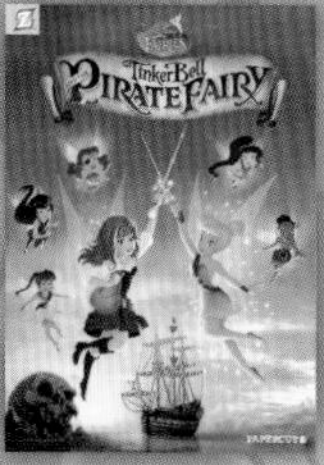

Graphic Novel #16
"Tinker Bell and the Pirate Fairy"

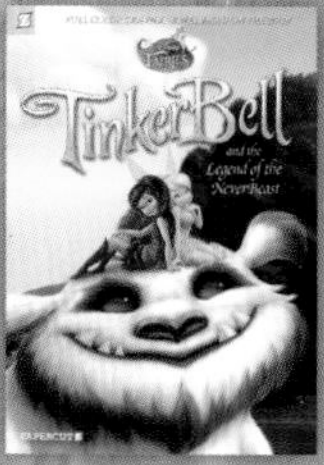

Graphic Novel #17
"Tinker Bell and the Legend of the NeverBeast"

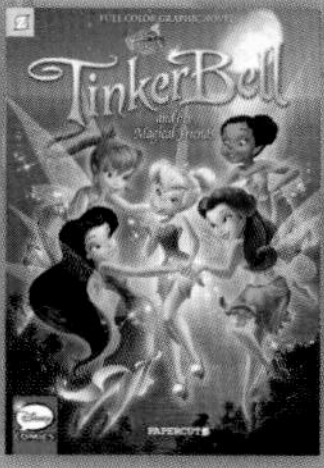

Graphic Novel #18
"Tinker Bell and her Magical Friends"

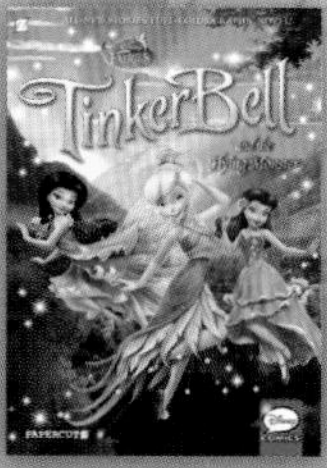

Graphic Novel #19
"Tinker Bell and the Flying Monster"

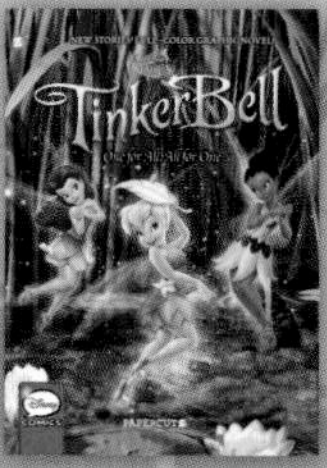

Graphic Novel #20
"Tinker Bell and a Far Too Secret Secret"

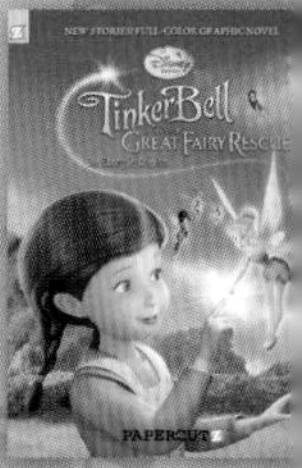

Tinker Bell and the Great Fairy Rescue

DISNEY FAIRIES graphic novels are available in paperback for $7.99 each; in hardcover for $12.99 each except #5, $6.99PB, $10.99HC, #6-14 are $7.99PB $11.99HC. Tinker Bell and the Great Fairy Rescue is $9.99 in hardcover on
Available at booksellers everywhere.

See more at papercutz.com

Or you can order from us: Please add $4.00 for postage and handling for first book, and add $1.00 for each additional book. Please make check payable to NBM Publishing. Send to: Papercutz, 160 Broadway, Suite 700, East Wing, New York, NY 10038 or call 800 886 1223 (9-6 EST M-F) MC-Visa-Amex accepted.

Disney FAIRIES

#20 "Tinker Bell and a Far-Too-Secret Secret"

Contents

PAPERCUTZ™
NEW YORK

Disney Fairies #20
"Tinker Bell and a Far-Too-Secret Secret"

"A Secret to Share"
Script: Tea Orsi
Layout and Cleanup: Emilio Grasso
Inks: Santa Zangari
Color: Studio Kawaii

"A Silver Lining"
Script: Emanuela Portipiano
Layout and Inks: Sara Storino
Cleanup: Marino Gentile
Color: Studio Kawaii

"Following A Dream"
Script: Carlo Panaro
Layout and Cleanup: Monica Catalano
Inks: Roberta Zanotta
Color: Studio Kawaii

"A Dazzling Delight"
Script: Emanuela Portipiano
Layout, Cleanup and Inks: Monica Catalano
Color: Studio Kawaii

"Water Games"
Script: Emanuela Portipiano
Layout, Cleanup and Inks: Monica Catalano
Color: Studio Kawaii

"A Far Too Secret Secret"
Script: Emanuela Portipiano
Layout: Emilio Grasso
Inks: Santa Zangari
Cleanup: Emilio Grasso and Marino Gentile
Color: Studio Kawaii

"A Question Of Taste"
Script: Emanuela Portipiano
Layout and Cleanup: Manuela Razzi
Inks: Santa Zangari
Color: Studio Kawaii

"One For All, All For One"
Script: Tea Orsi
Layout, Cleanup and Inks: Sara Storino
Color: Studio Kawaii

"The Difficult Delivery"
Script: Tea Orsi
Layout and Cleanup: Sara Storino
Inks: Santa Zangari
Color: Studio Kawaii

"Mushroom Mayhem"
Script: Tea Orsi
Layout and Cleanup: Marino Gentile
Inks: Roberta Zanotta
Color: Studio Kawaii

"Perfumed and Perfect"
Script: Tea Orsi
Layout: Sara Storino
Inks: Santa Zangari
Cleanup: Marino Gentile
Color: Studio Kawaii

"Good Night, Bunny!"
Script: Tea Orsi
Layout and Cleanup: Marino Gentile
Inks: Santa Zangari
Color: Studio Kawaii

"Cooking Talent?"
Script: De Cunto Marta
Layout and Cleanup: Barone Gianlu
Inks: Santa Zangari
Color: Studio Kawaii

"A Little Nap"
Script: Silvia Lombardi
Layout and Cleanup: Sara Storino
Inks: Santa Zangari
Color: Studio Kawaii

Minnie & Daisy #2 Preview
Script: Silvia Gianatti
Art: Stefano De Lellis
Inks: Santa Zangari
Color: Angela Capolupo

Production – Dawn Guzzo
Production Coordinator – Sasha Kimiatek
Editor – Robert V. Conte
Assistant Managing Editor – Jeff Whitman
Special Thanks to – Carlotta Quattrocolo, Arianna Marchione, Krista Wong, and Eugene Paraszczuk at Disney Enterprises, Inc
Jim Salicrup
Editor-in-Chief

ISBN: 978-1-62991-784-9 Paperback Edition
ISBN: 978-1-62991-785-6 Hardcover Edition

Printed in Korea
Printed April 2017

Papercutz books may be purchased for business or promotional use.
For information on bulk purchases please contact Macmillan
Corporate and Premium Sales Department at (800) 221-7945 x5442.

Distributed by Macmillan
First Papercutz Printing

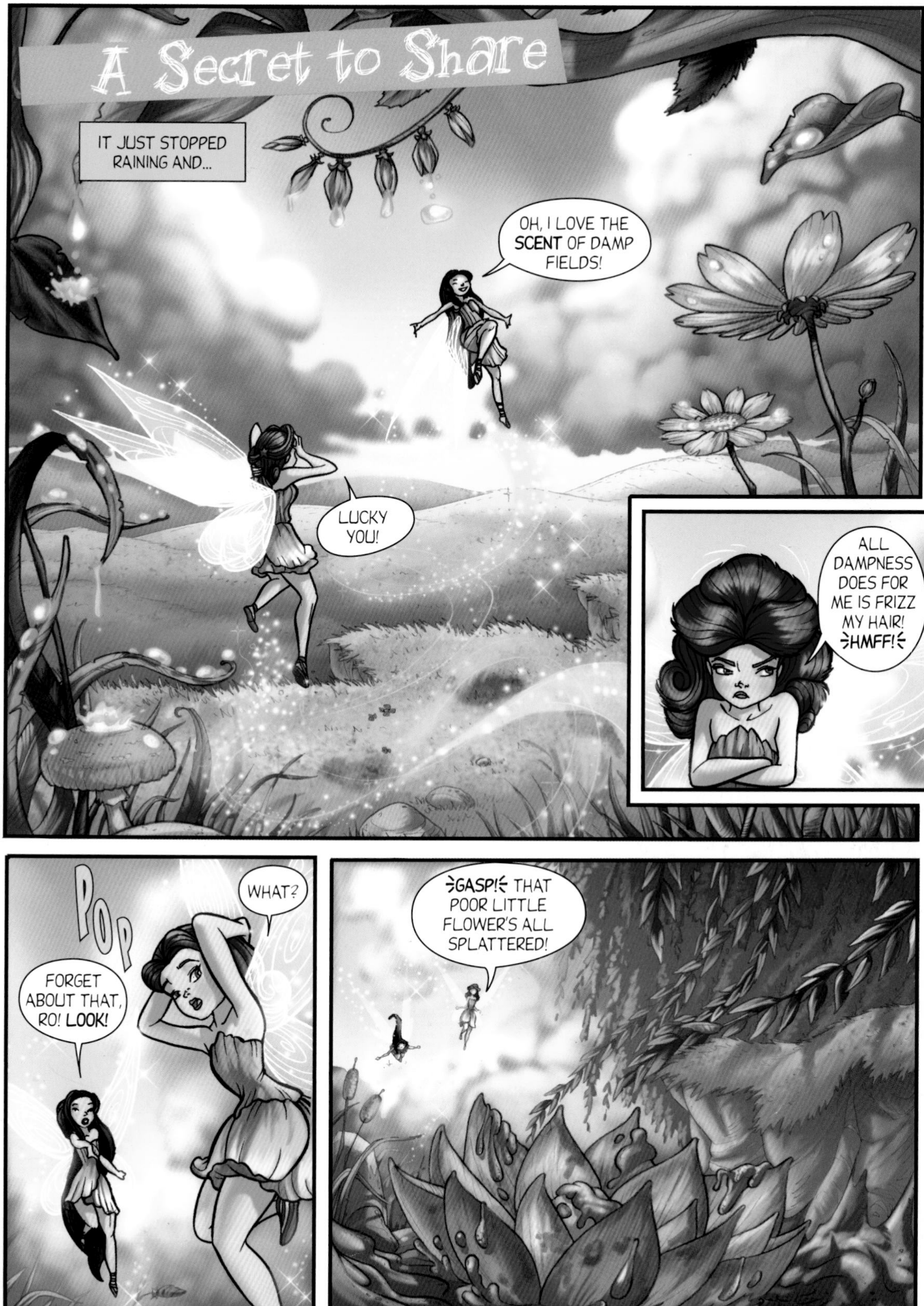
A Secret to Share
IT JUST STOPPED RAINING AND...
OH, I LOVE THE SCENT OF DAMP FIELDS!
LUCKY YOU!
ALL DAMPNESS DOES FOR ME IS FRIZZ MY HAIR! HMFF!
POP
WHAT?
FORGET ABOUT THAT, RO! LOOK!
GASP! THAT POOR LITTLE FLOWER'S ALL SPLATTERED!

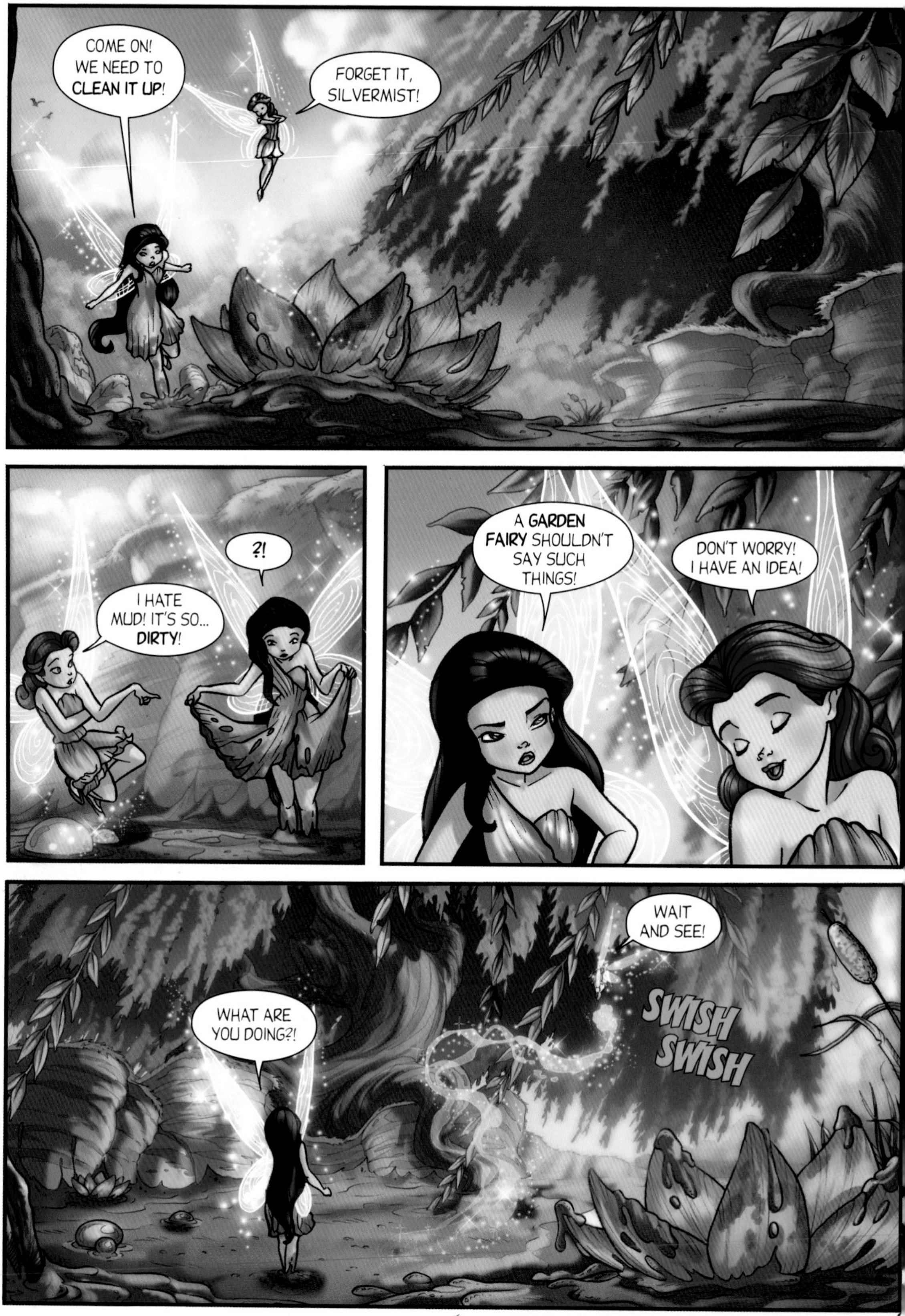
COME ON! WE NEED TO CLEAN IT UP!
FORGET IT, SILVERMIST!
?!
I HATE MUD! IT'S SO... DIRTY!
A GARDEN FAIRY SHOULDN'T SAY SUCH THINGS!
DON'T WORRY! I HAVE AN IDEA!
WAIT AND SEE!
WHAT ARE YOU DOING?!
SWISH SWISH

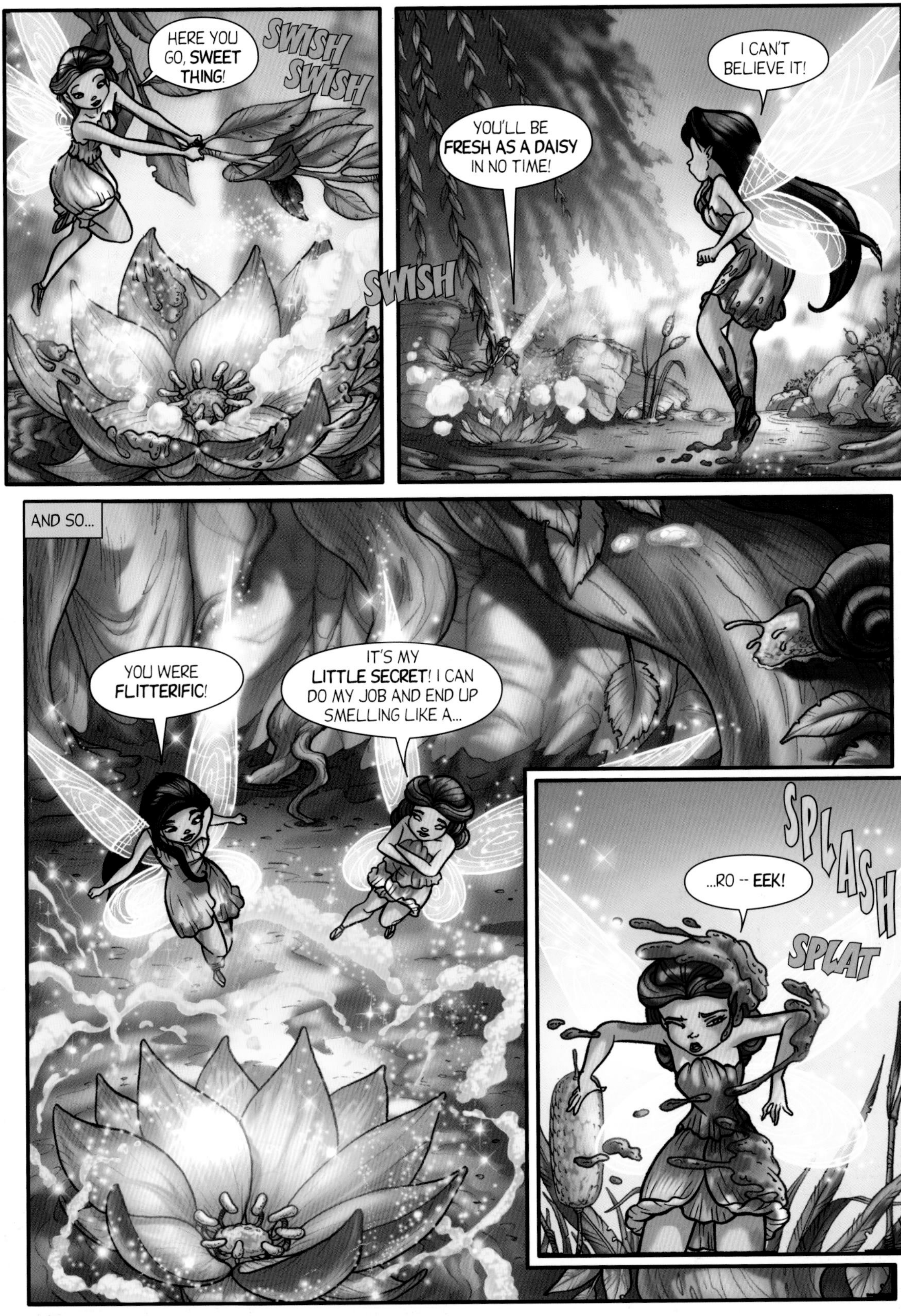
HERE YOU GO, **SWEET THING**!
SWISH SWISH
I CAN'T BELIEVE IT!
YOU'LL BE **FRESH AS A DAISY** IN NO TIME!
SWISH
AND SO...
YOU WERE **FLITTERIFIC**!
IT'S MY **LITTLE SECRET**! I CAN DO MY JOB AND END UP SMELLING LIKE A...
SPLASH
...RO -- **EEK!**
SPLAT

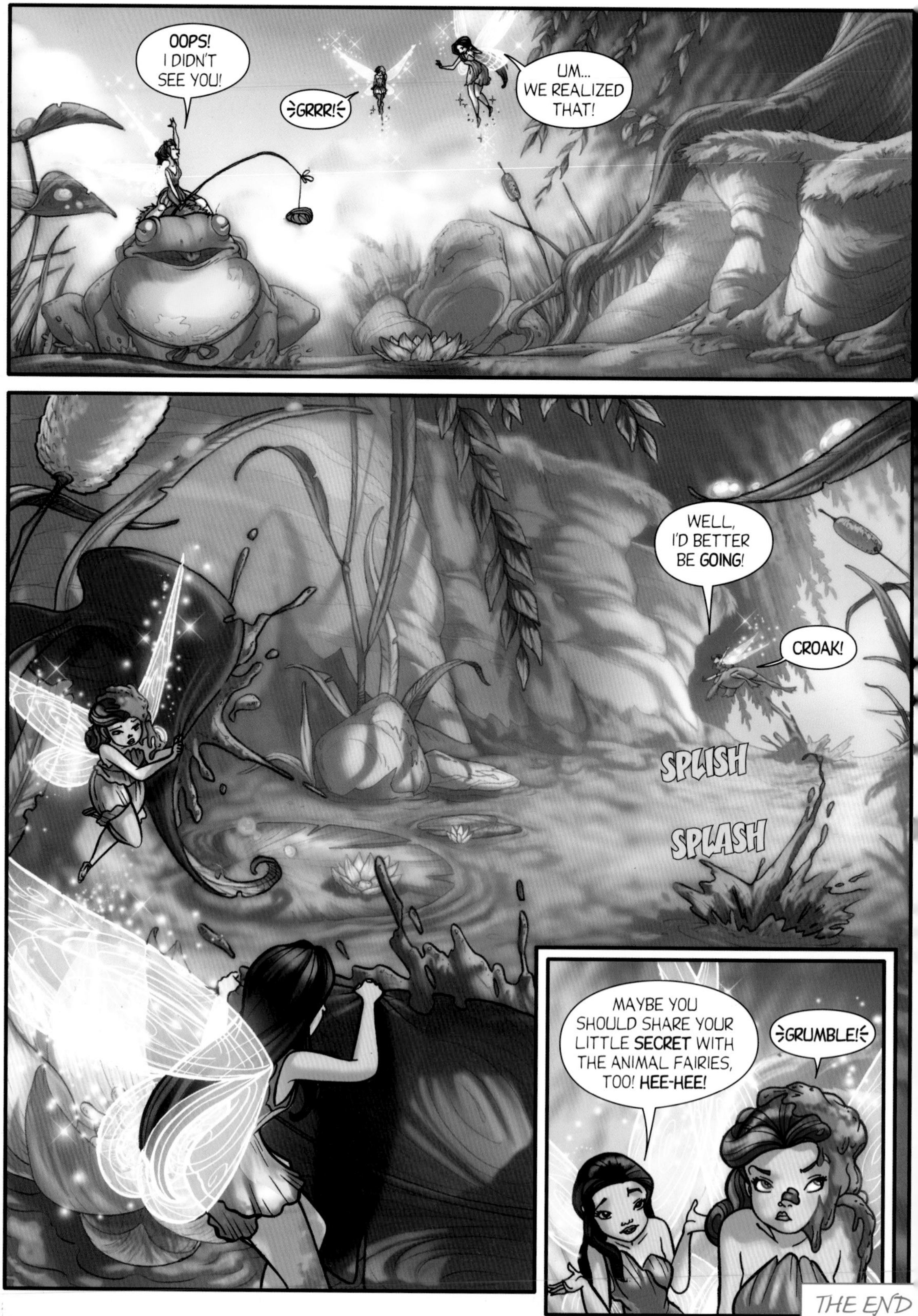
OOPS! I DIDN'T SEE YOU!
GRRR!
UM... WE REALIZED THAT!
WELL, I'D BETTER BE GOING!
CROAK!
SPLISH
SPLASH
MAYBE YOU SHOULD SHARE YOUR LITTLE SECRET WITH THE ANIMAL FAIRIES, TOO! HEE-HEE!
GRUMBLE!
THE END

A Silver Lining

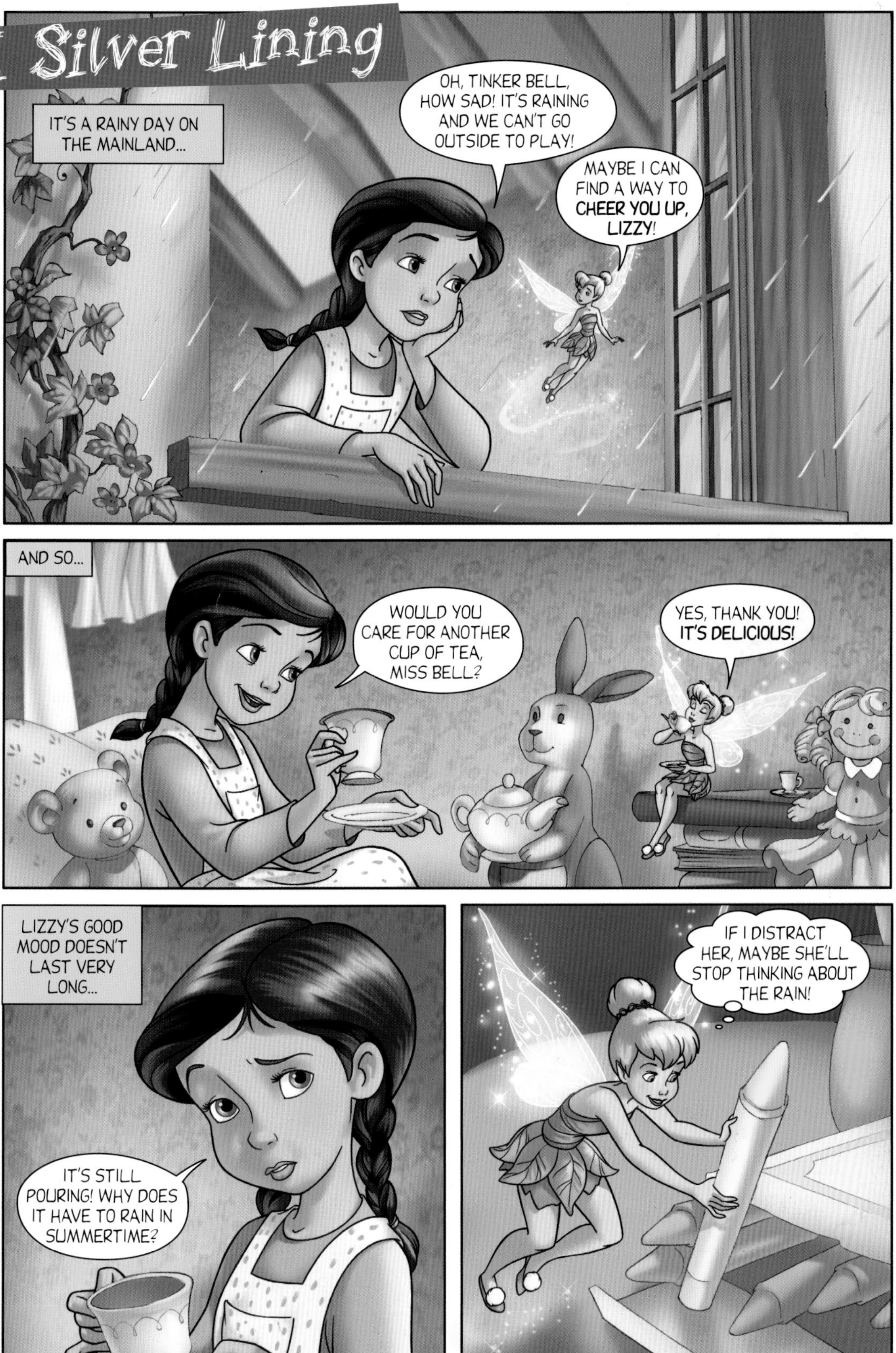

IT'S A RAINY DAY ON THE MAINLAND...
OH, TINKER BELL, HOW SAD! IT'S RAINING AND WE CAN'T GO OUTSIDE TO PLAY!
MAYBE I CAN FIND A WAY TO **CHEER YOU UP, LIZZY**!
AND SO...
WOULD YOU CARE FOR ANOTHER CUP OF TEA, MISS BELL?
YES, THANK YOU! **IT'S DELICIOUS!**
LIZZY'S GOOD MOOD DOESN'T LAST VERY LONG...
IT'S STILL POURING! WHY DOES IT HAVE TO RAIN IN SUMMERTIME?
IF I DISTRACT HER, MAYBE SHE'LL STOP THINKING ABOUT THE RAIN!

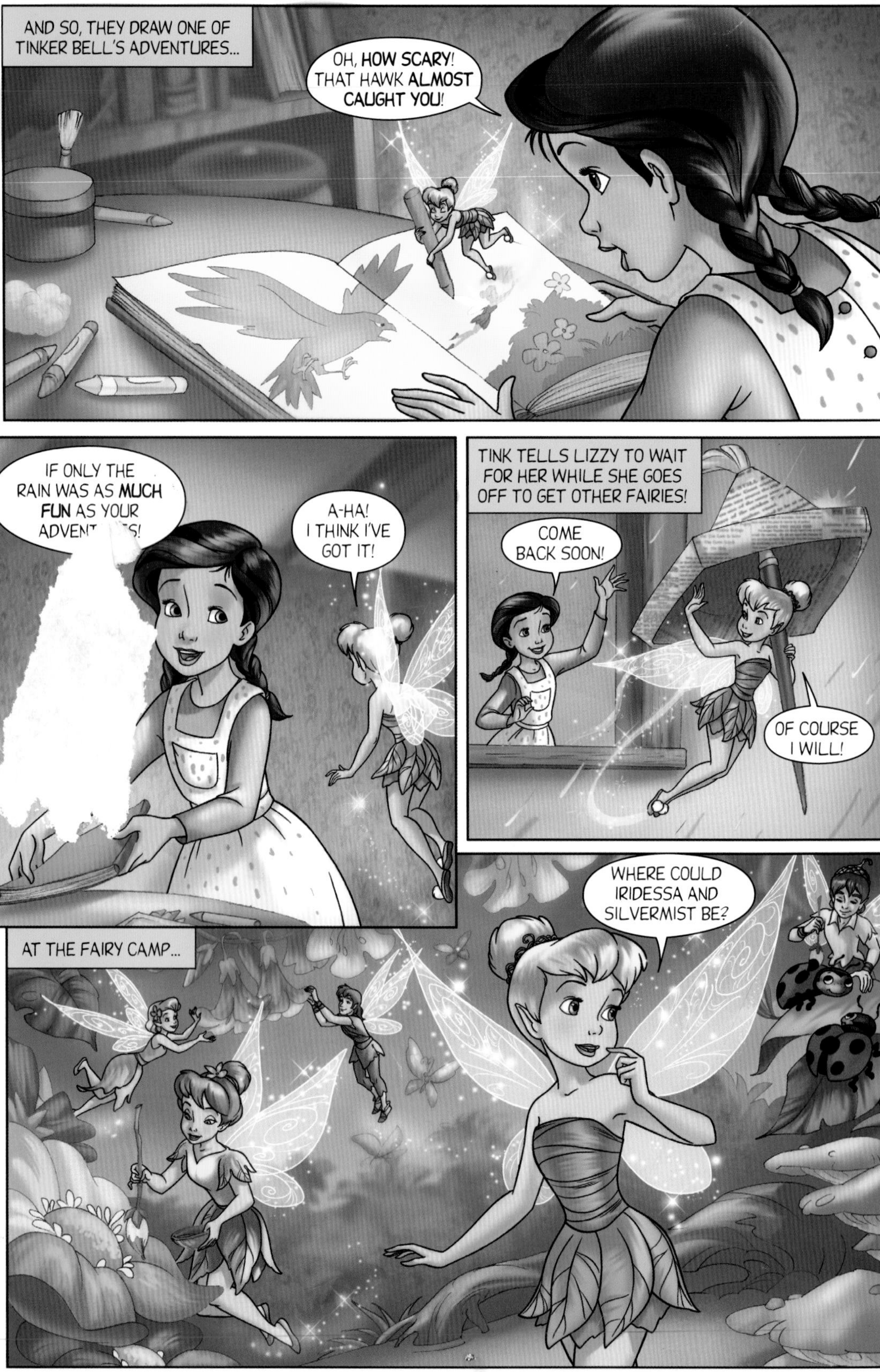
AND SO, THEY DRAW ONE OF TINKER BELL'S ADVENTURES...
OH, **HOW SCARY**! THAT HAWK **ALMOST CAUGHT YOU**!
IF ONLY THE RAIN WAS AS **MUCH FUN** AS YOUR ADVENT ES!
A-HA! I THINK I'VE GOT IT!
TINK TELLS LIZZY TO WAIT FOR HER WHILE SHE GOES OFF TO GET OTHER FAIRIES!
COME BACK SOON!
OF COURSE I WILL!
AT THE FAIRY CAMP...
WHERE COULD IRIDESSA AND SILVERMIST BE?

- 11 -

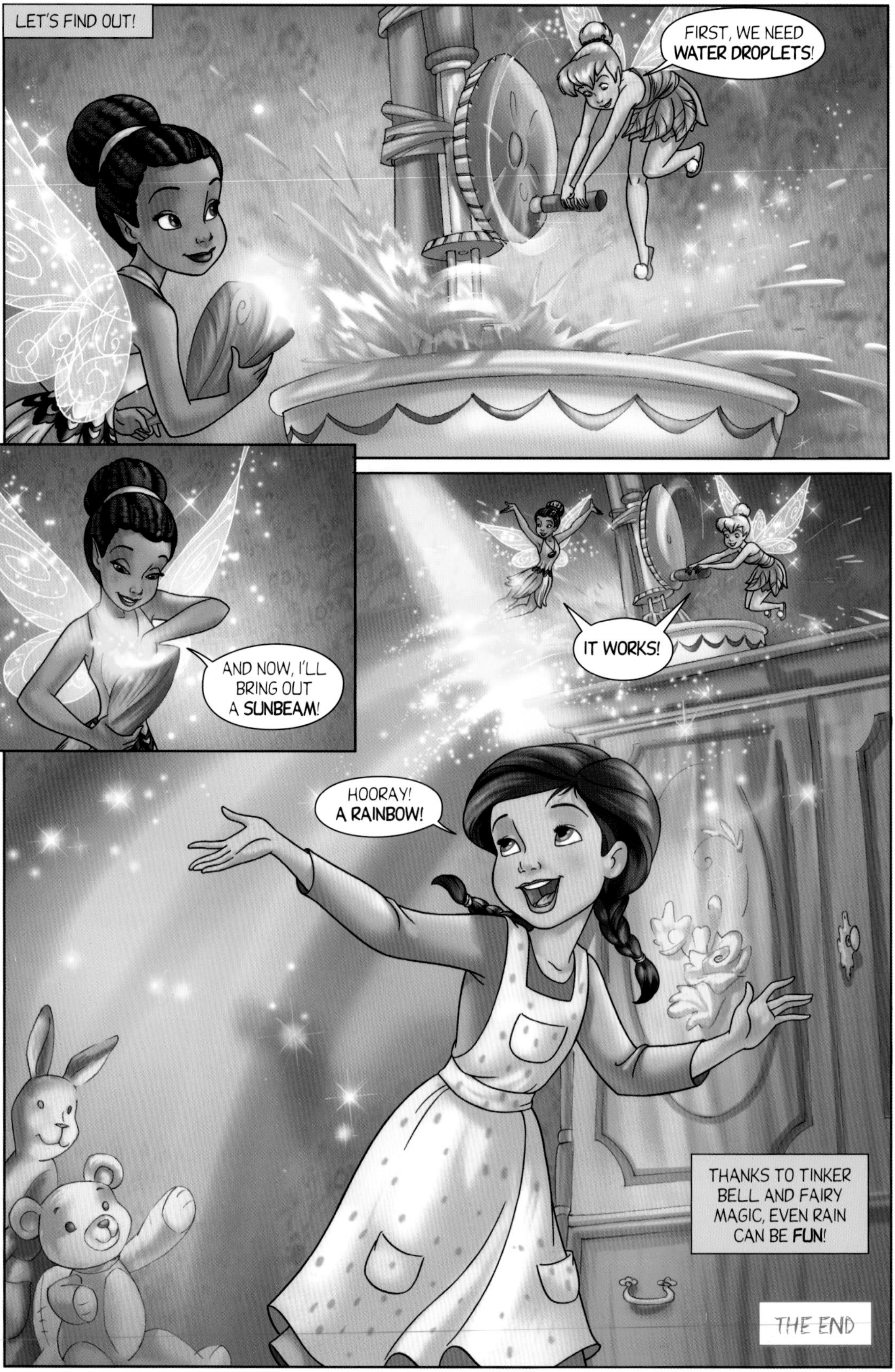
LET'S FIND OUT!
FIRST, WE NEED WATER DROPLETS!
AND NOW, I'LL BRING OUT A SUNBEAM!
IT WORKS!
HOORAY! A RAINBOW!
THANKS TO TINKER BELL AND FAIRY MAGIC, EVEN RAIN CAN BE FUN!
THE END

Following a Dream

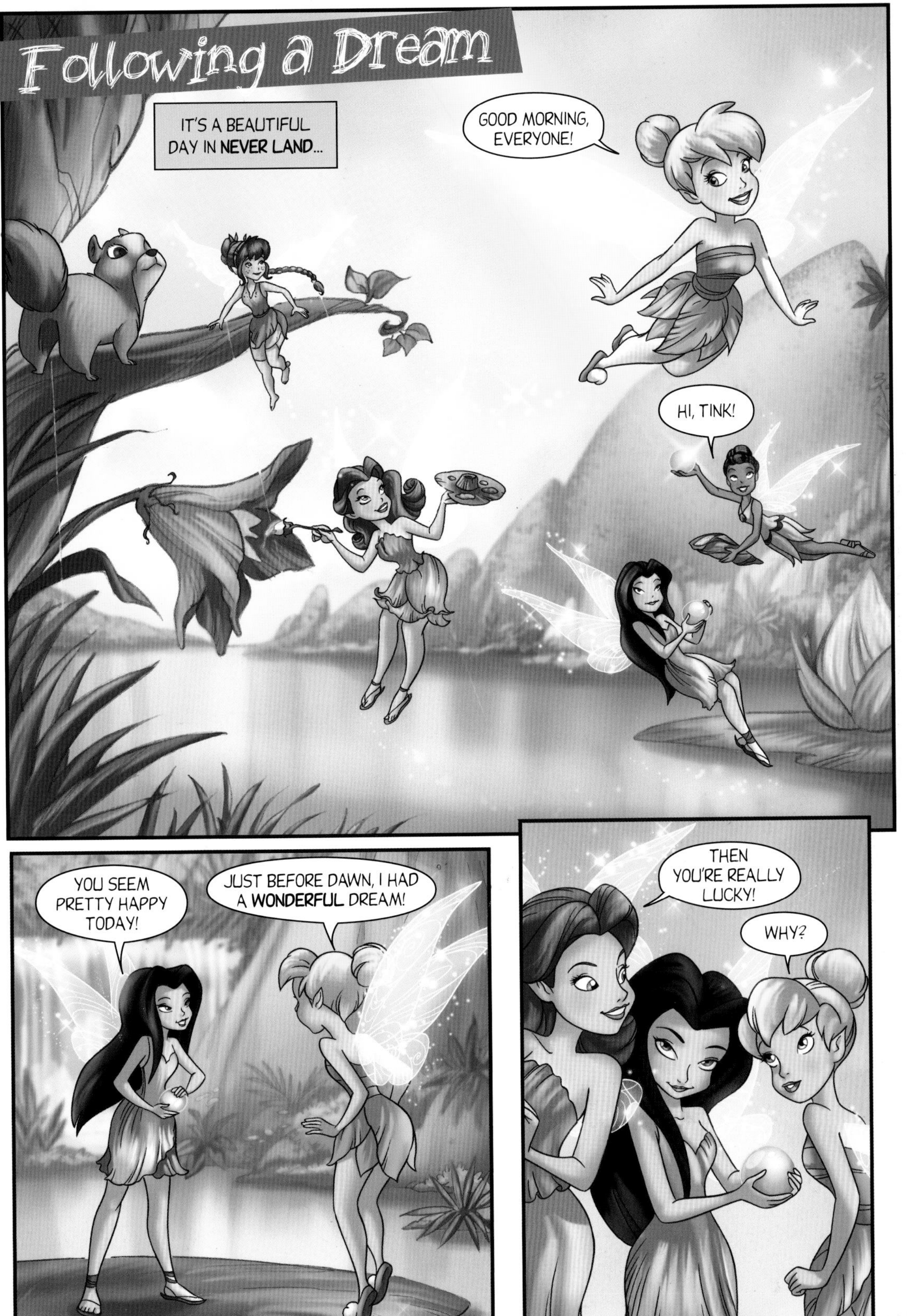
IT'S A BEAUTIFUL DAY IN **NEVER LAND**...
GOOD MORNING, EVERYONE!
HI, TINK!
YOU SEEM PRETTY HAPPY TODAY!
JUST BEFORE DAWN, I HAD A **WONDERFUL** DREAM!
THEN YOU'RE REALLY LUCKY!
WHY?

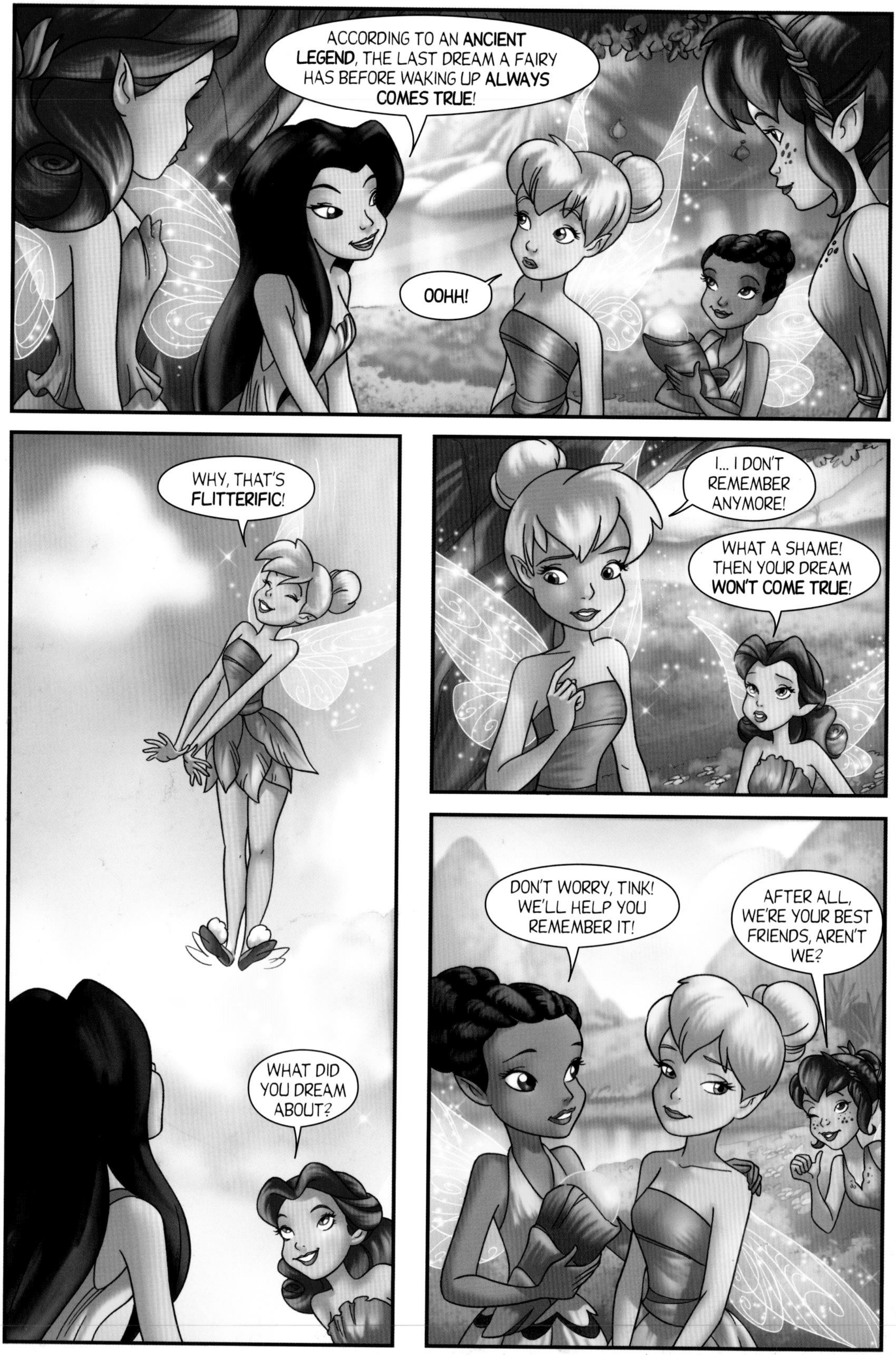

ACCORDING TO AN ANCIENT LEGEND, THE LAST DREAM A FAIRY HAS BEFORE WAKING UP ALWAYS COMES TRUE!
OOHH!
WHY, THAT'S FLITTERIFIC!
WHAT DID YOU DREAM ABOUT?
I... I DON'T REMEMBER ANYMORE!
WHAT A SHAME! THEN YOUR DREAM WON'T COME TRUE!
DON'T WORRY, TINK! WE'LL HELP YOU REMEMBER IT!
AFTER ALL, WE'RE YOUR BEST FRIENDS, AREN'T WE?

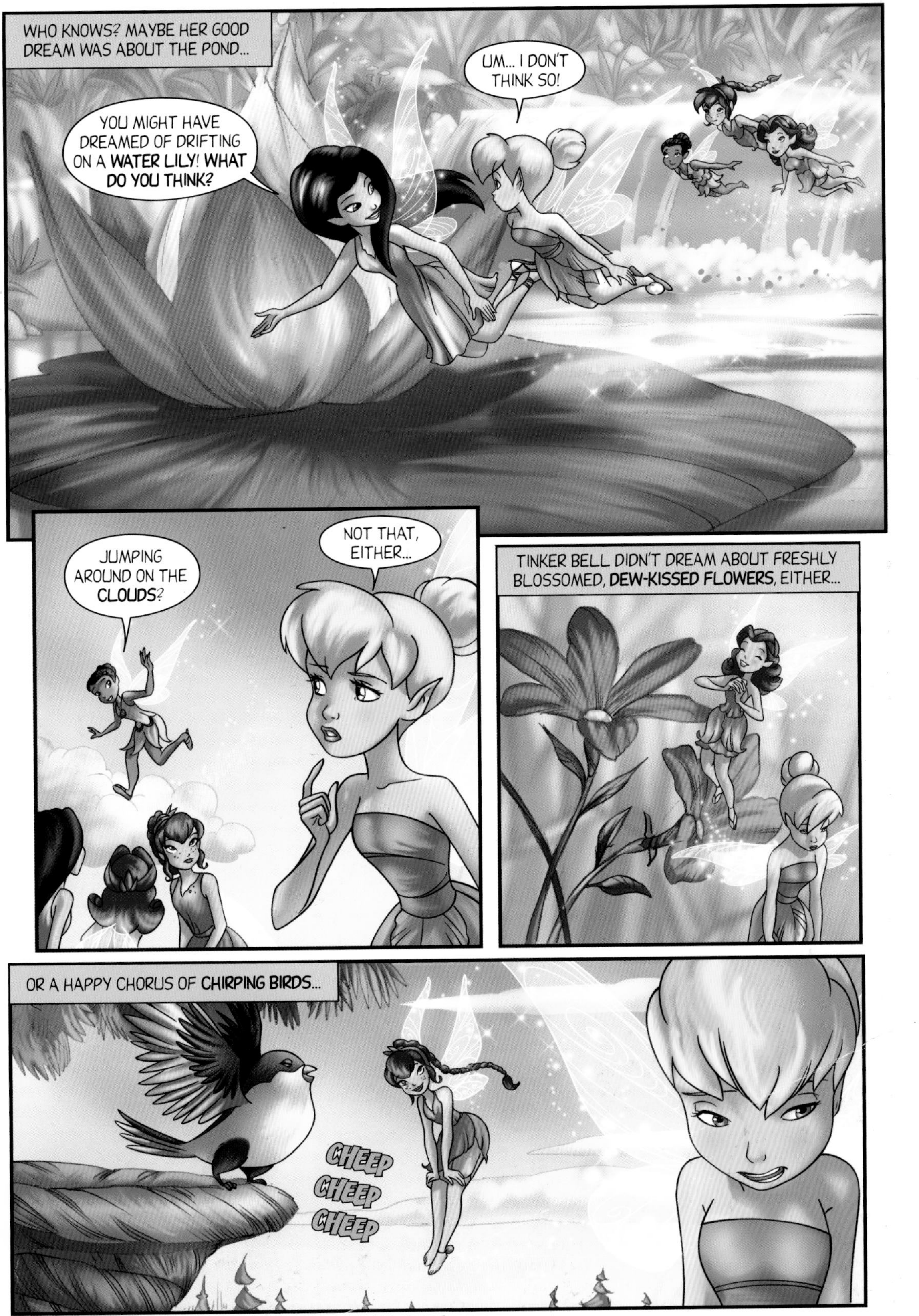
WHO KNOWS? MAYBE HER GOOD DREAM WAS ABOUT THE POND...
YOU MIGHT HAVE DREAMED OF DRIFTING ON A **WATER LILY! WHAT DO YOU THINK?**
UM... I DON'T THINK SO!
JUMPING AROUND ON THE **CLOUDS**?
NOT THAT, EITHER...
TINKER BELL DIDN'T DREAM ABOUT FRESHLY BLOSSOMED, **DEW-KISSED FLOWERS**, EITHER...
OR A HAPPY CHORUS OF **CHIRPING BIRDS**...
CHEEP
CHEEP
CHEEP

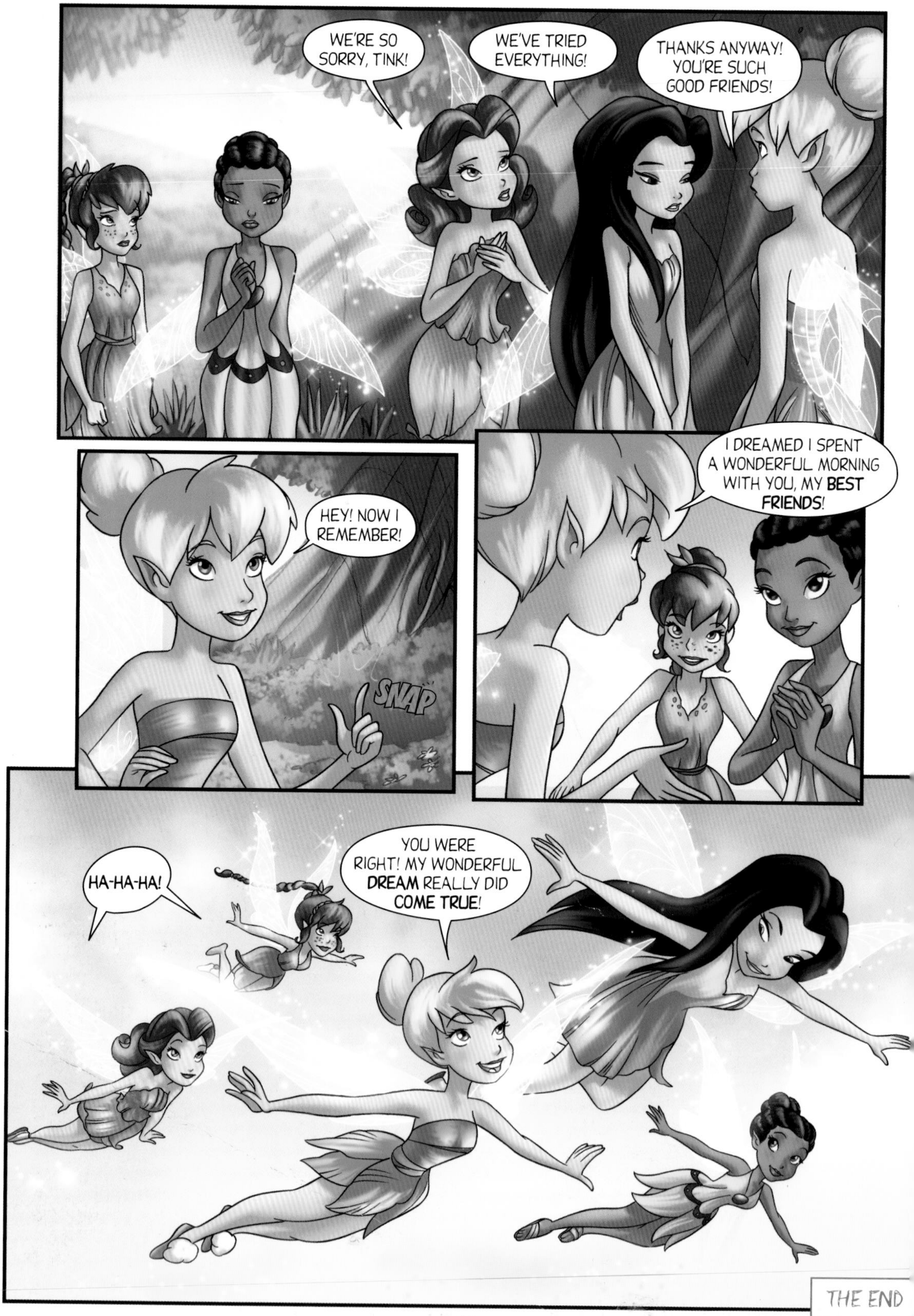
WE'RE SO SORRY, TINK!
WE'VE TRIED EVERYTHING!
THANKS ANYWAY! YOU'RE SUCH GOOD FRIENDS!
HEY! NOW I REMEMBER!
SNAP
I DREAMED I SPENT A WONDERFUL MORNING WITH YOU, MY **BEST FRIENDS**!
HA-HA-HA!
YOU WERE RIGHT! MY WONDERFUL **DREAM** REALLY DID **COME TRUE**!
THE END

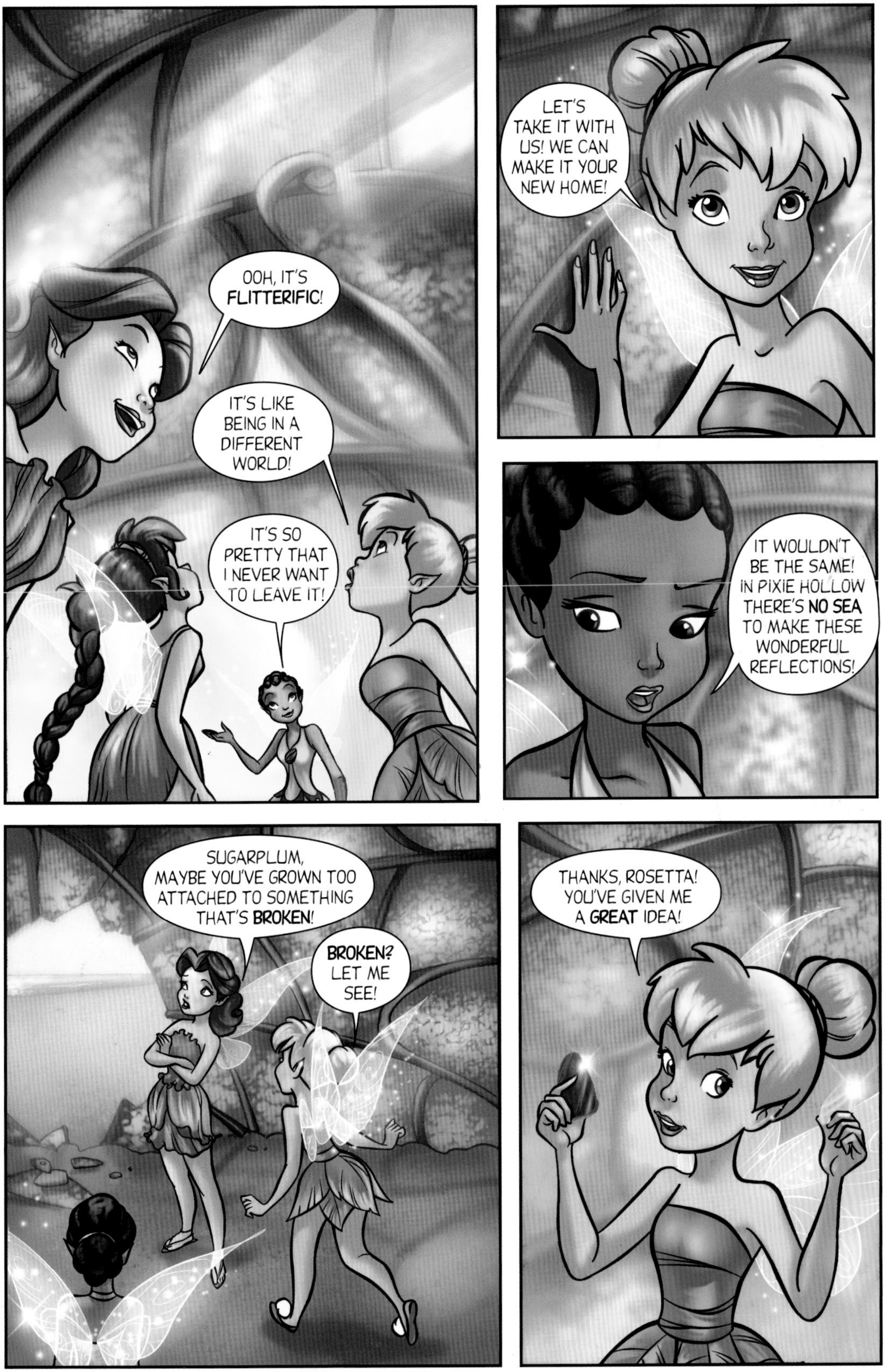
OOH, IT'S **FLITTERIFIC**!
IT'S LIKE BEING IN A DIFFERENT WORLD!
IT'S SO PRETTY THAT I NEVER WANT TO LEAVE IT!
LET'S TAKE IT WITH US! WE CAN MAKE IT YOUR NEW HOME!
IT WOULDN'T BE THE SAME! IN PIXIE HOLLOW THERE'S **NO SEA** TO MAKE THESE WONDERFUL REFLECTIONS!
SUGARPLUM, MAYBE YOU'VE GROWN TOO ATTACHED TO SOMETHING THAT'S **BROKEN**!
BROKEN? LET ME SEE!
THANKS, ROSETTA! YOU'VE GIVEN ME A **GREAT** IDEA!

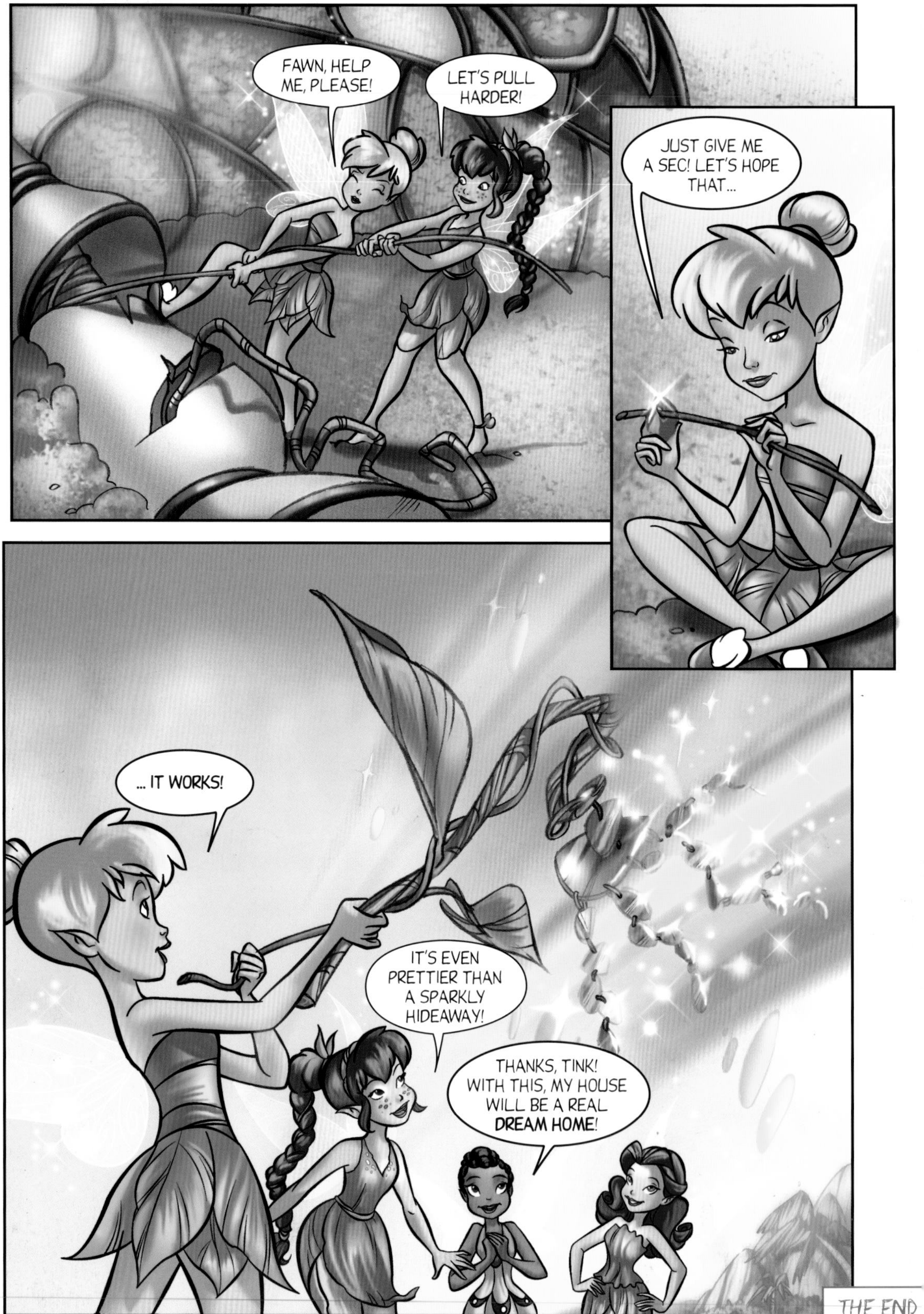
FAWN, HELP ME, PLEASE!
LET'S PULL HARDER!
JUST GIVE ME A SEC! LET'S HOPE THAT...
... IT WORKS!
IT'S EVEN PRETTIER THAN A SPARKLY HIDEAWAY!
THANKS, TINK! WITH THIS, MY HOUSE WILL BE A REAL DREAM HOME!
THE END

Water Games

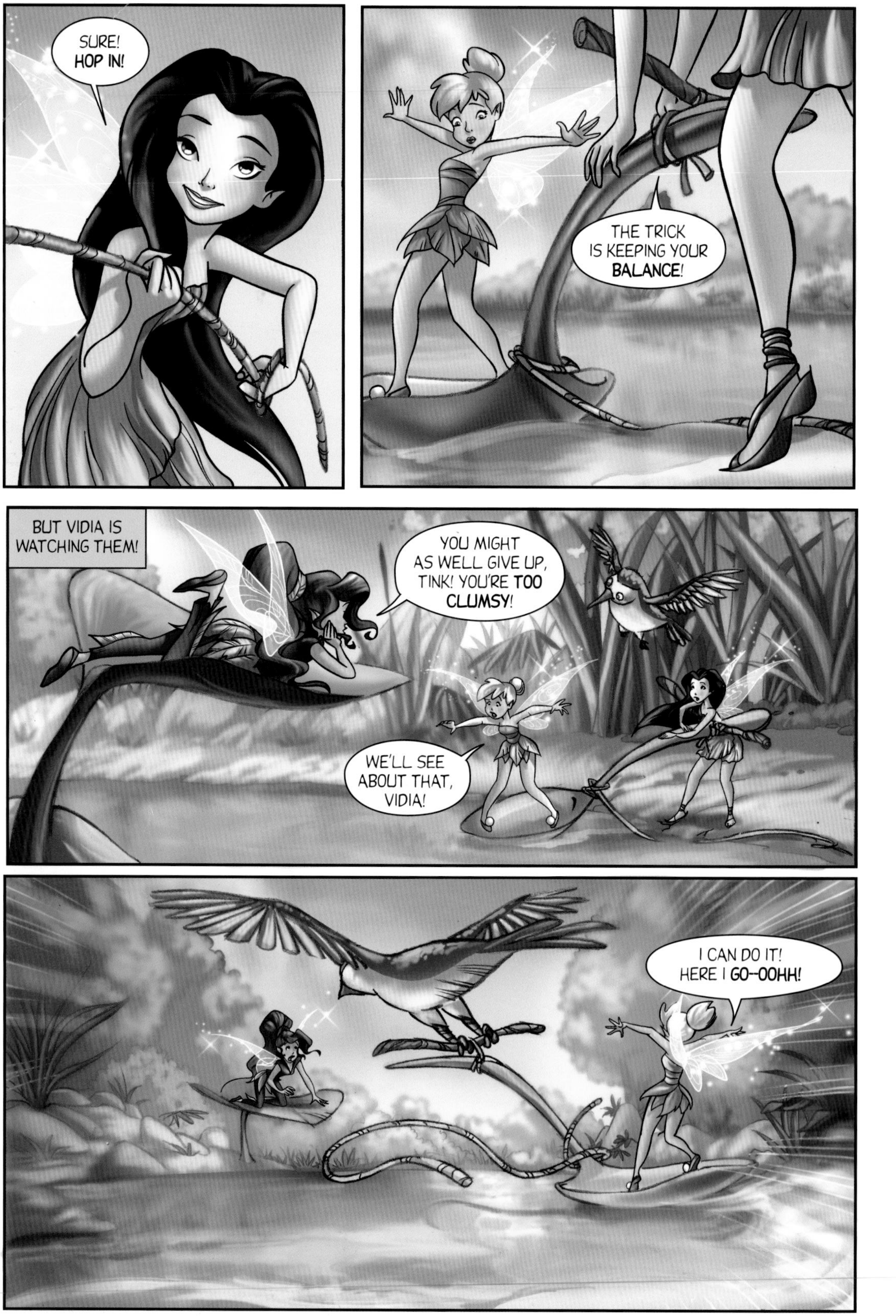

SURE! HOP IN!
THE TRICK IS KEEPING YOUR BALANCE!
BUT VIDIA IS WATCHING THEM!
YOU MIGHT AS WELL GIVE UP, TINK! YOU'RE TOO CLUMSY!
WE'LL SEE ABOUT THAT, VIDIA!
I CAN DO IT! HERE I GO--OOHH!

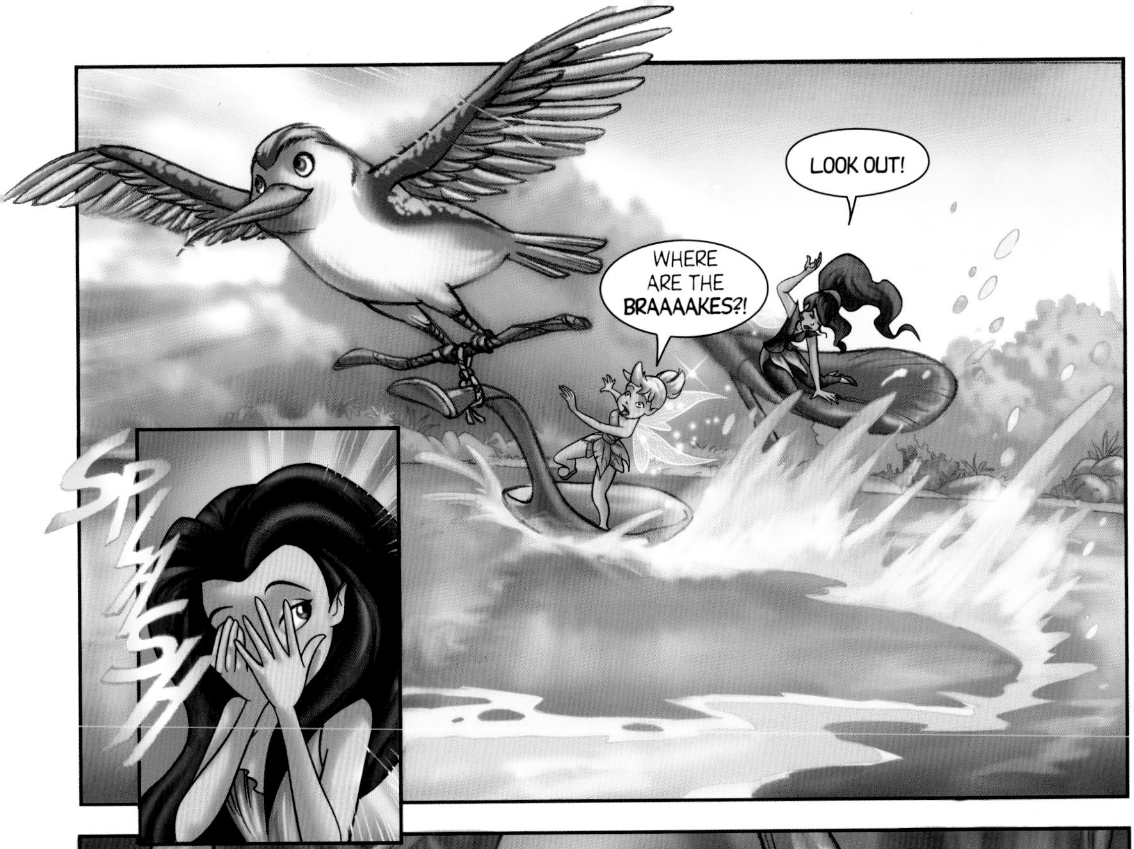
SPLASH
WHERE ARE THE BRAAAAKES?!
LOOK OUT!

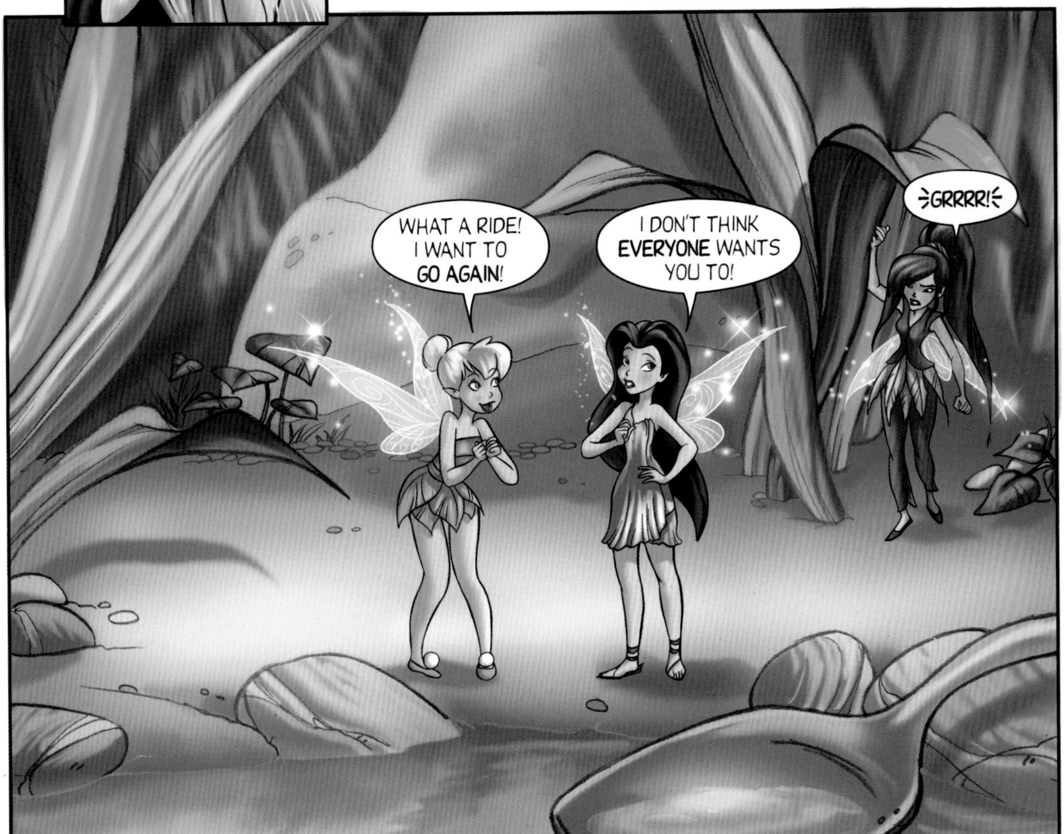
WHAT A RIDE! I WANT TO GO AGAIN!
I DON'T THINK EVERYONE WANTS YOU TO!
GRRRR!

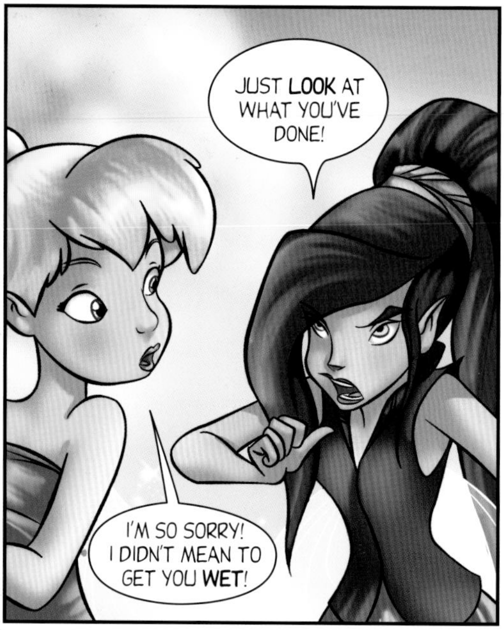
JUST **LOOK** AT WHAT YOU'VE DONE!
I'M SO SORRY! I DIDN'T MEAN TO GET YOU **WET**!

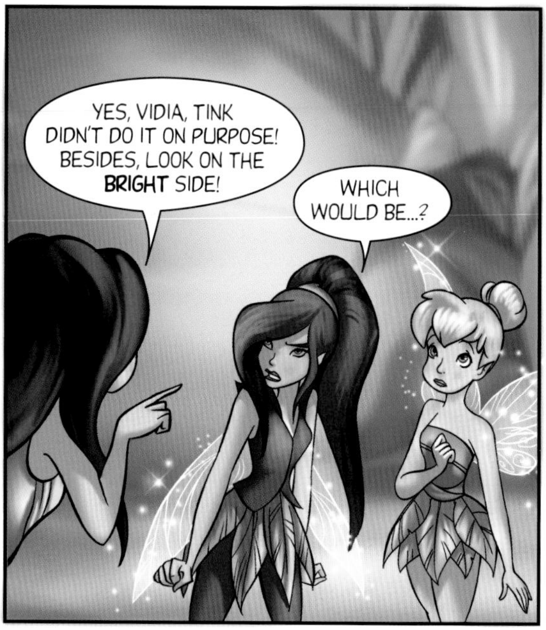
YES, VIDIA, TINK DIDN'T DO IT ON PURPOSE! BESIDES, LOOK ON THE **BRIGHT** SIDE!
WHICH WOULD BE...?

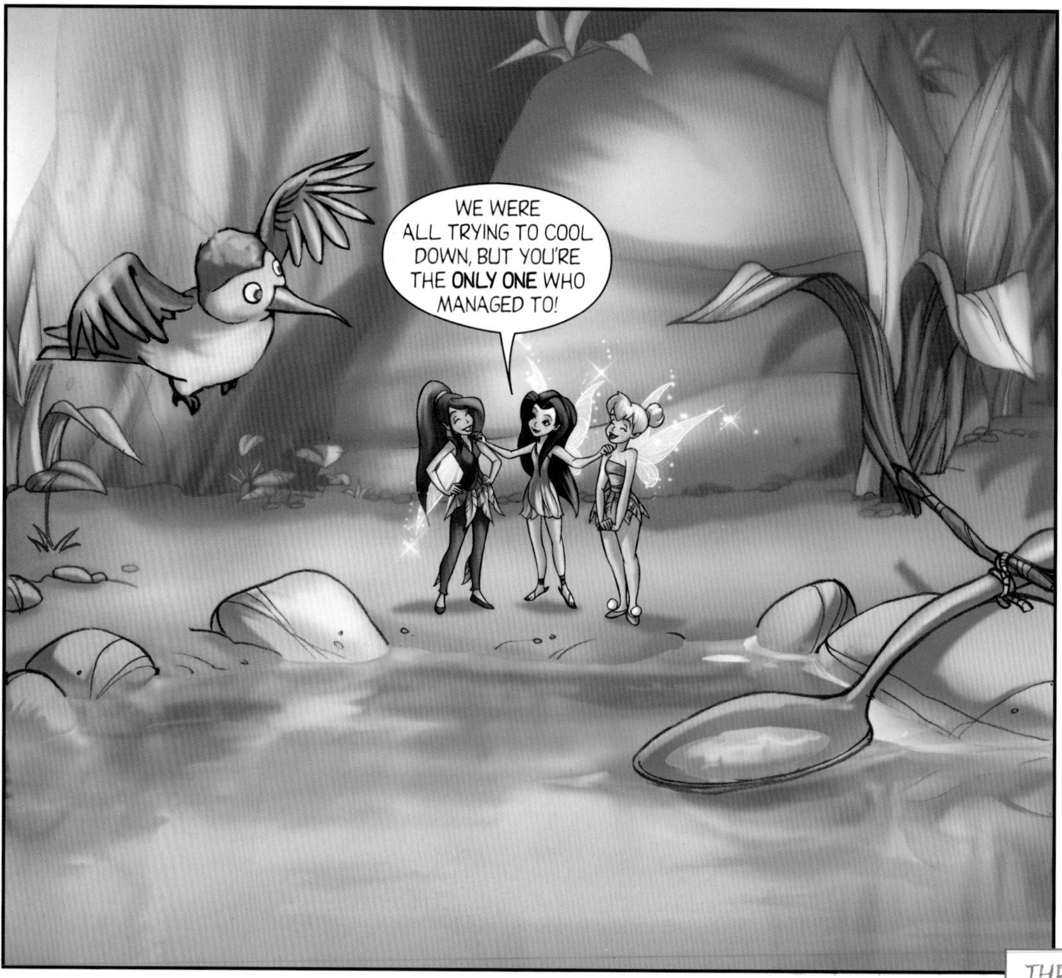
WE WERE ALL TRYING TO COOL DOWN, BUT YOU'RE THE **ONLY ONE** WHO MANAGED TO!

THE END

- 26 -

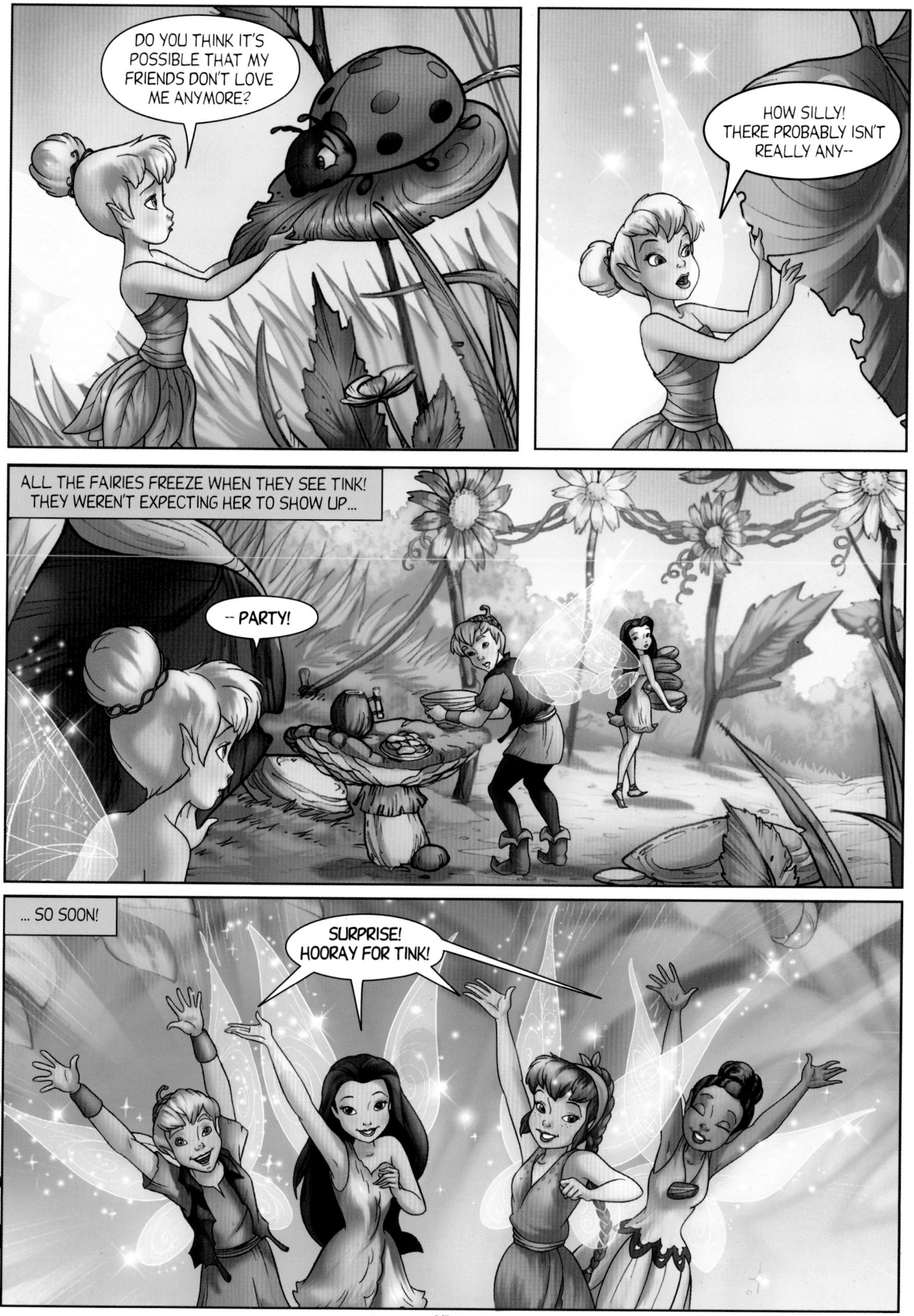
DO YOU THINK IT'S POSSIBLE THAT MY FRIENDS DON'T LOVE ME ANYMORE?
HOW SILLY! THERE PROBABLY ISN'T REALLY ANY--
ALL THE FAIRIES FREEZE WHEN THEY SEE TINK! THEY WEREN'T EXPECTING HER TO SHOW UP...
-- PARTY!
... SO SOON!
SURPRISE! HOORAY FOR TINK!

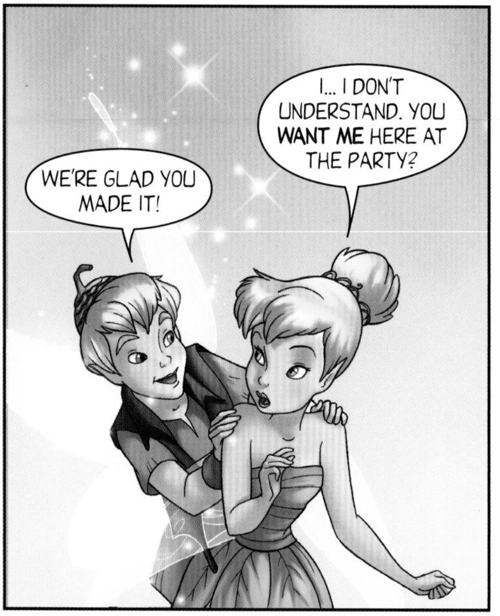
WE'RE GLAD YOU MADE IT!
I... I DON'T UNDERSTAND. YOU WANT ME HERE AT THE PARTY?

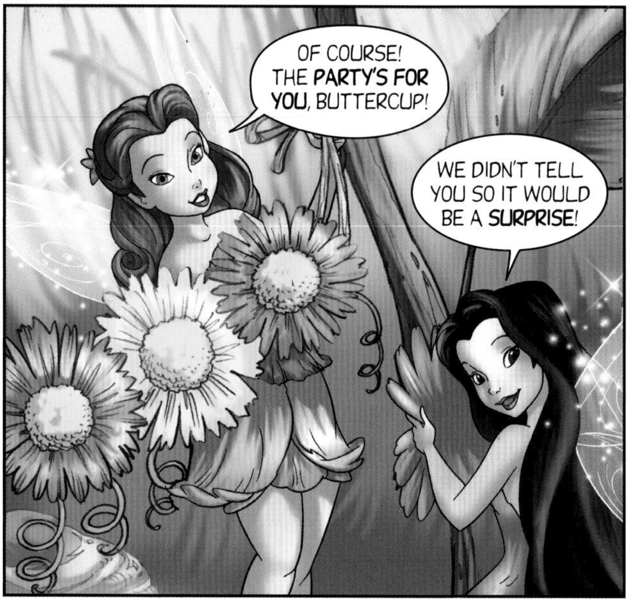
OF COURSE! THE PARTY'S FOR YOU, BUTTERCUP!
WE DIDN'T TELL YOU SO IT WOULD BE A SURPRISE!

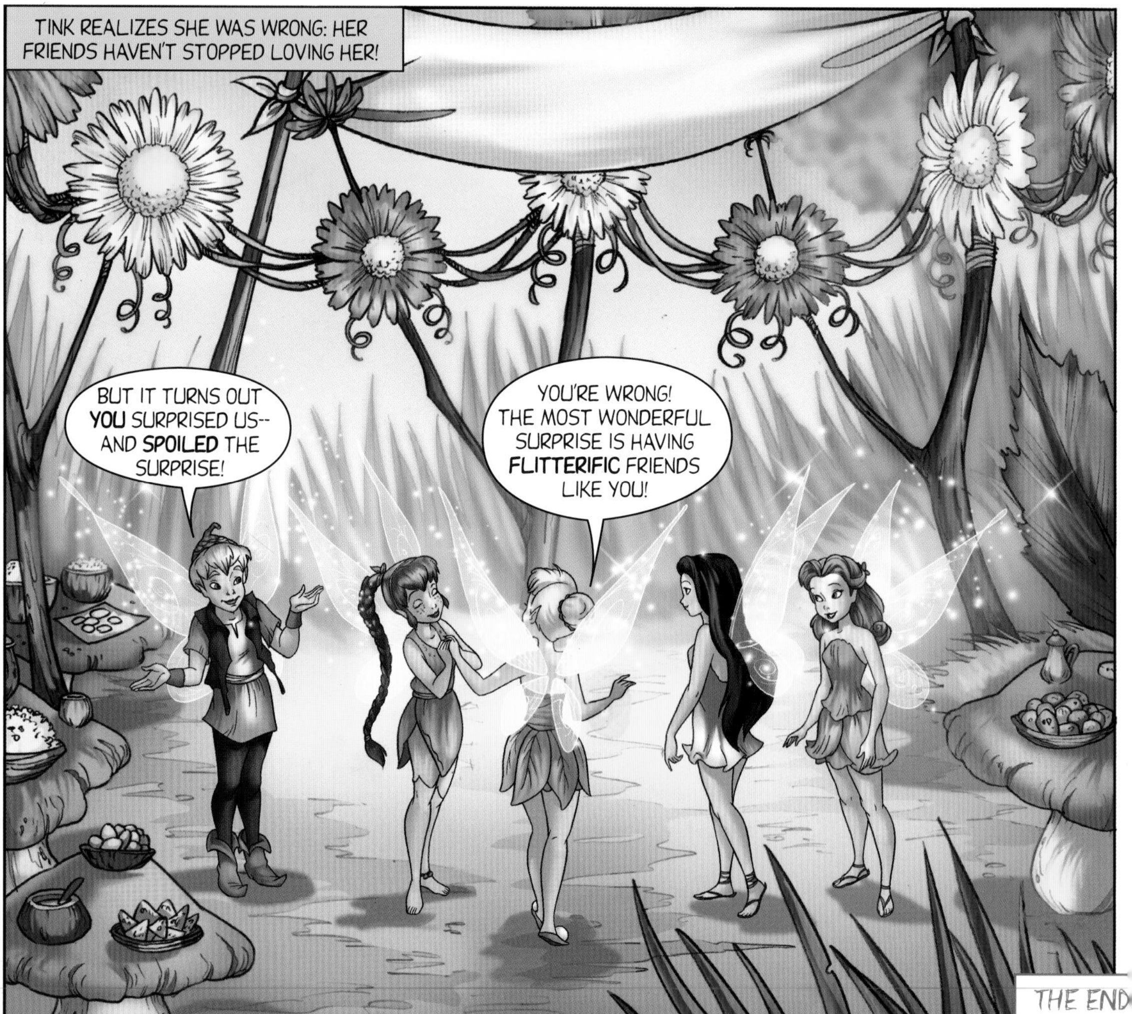
TINK REALIZES SHE WAS WRONG: HER FRIENDS HAVEN'T STOPPED LOVING HER!
BUT IT TURNS OUT YOU SURPRISED US-- AND SPOILED THE SURPRISE!
YOU'RE WRONG! THE MOST WONDERFUL SURPRISE IS HAVING FLITTERIFIC FRIENDS LIKE YOU!
THE END

A Question of Taste!

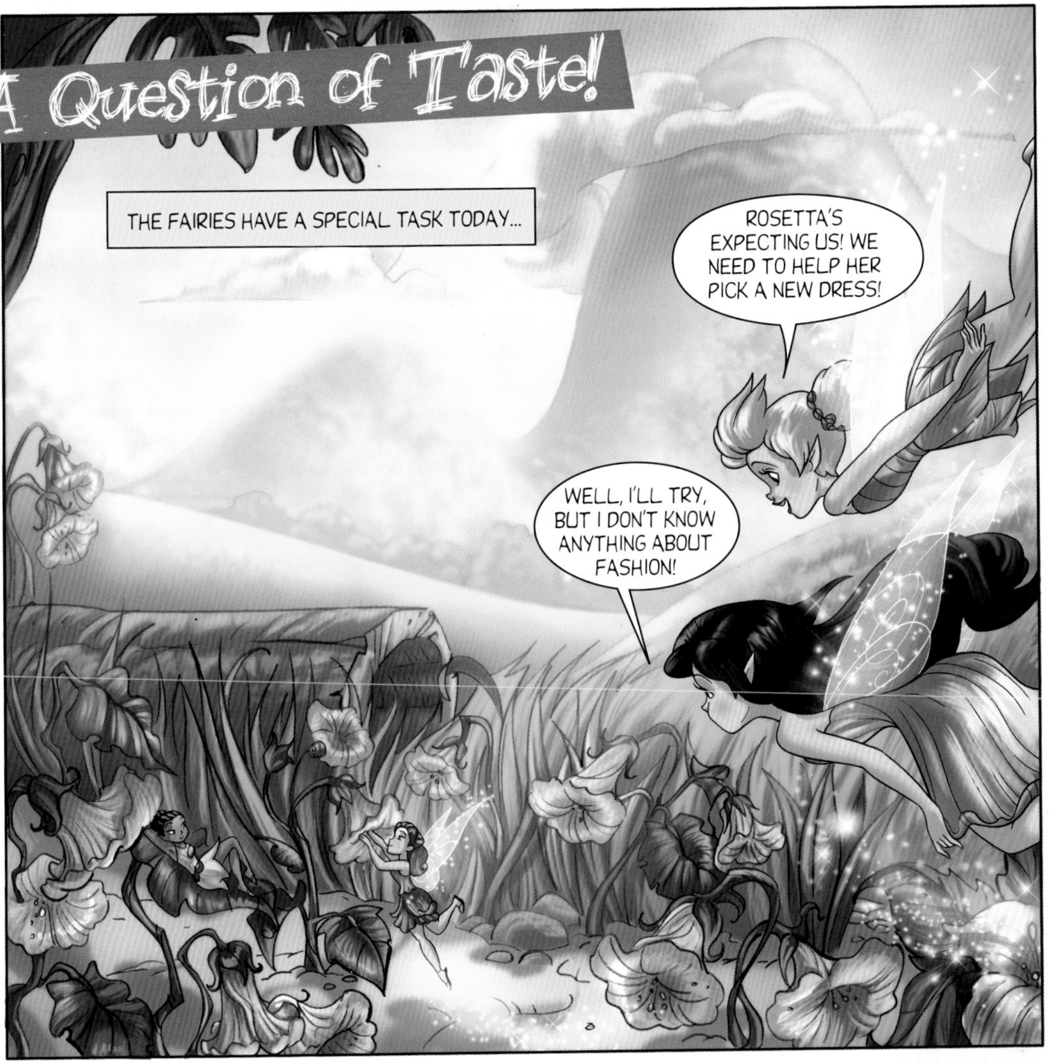
THE FAIRIES HAVE A SPECIAL TASK TODAY...
ROSETTA'S EXPECTING US! WE NEED TO HELP HER PICK A NEW DRESS!
WELL, I'LL TRY, BUT I DON'T KNOW ANYTHING ABOUT FASHION!

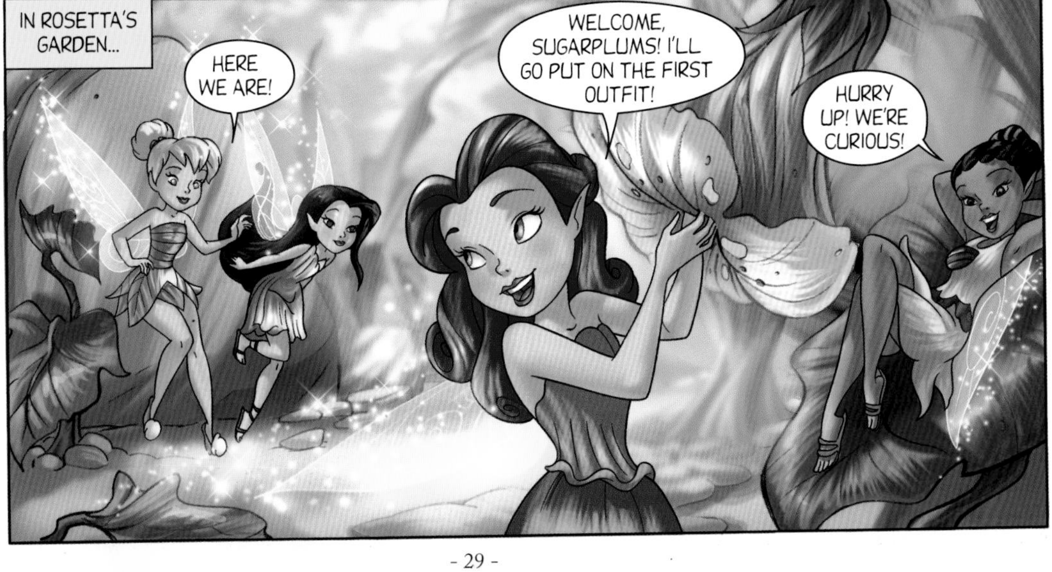
IN ROSETTA'S GARDEN...
HERE WE ARE!
WELCOME, SUGARPLUMS! I'LL GO PUT ON THE FIRST OUTFIT!
HURRY UP! WE'RE CURIOUS!

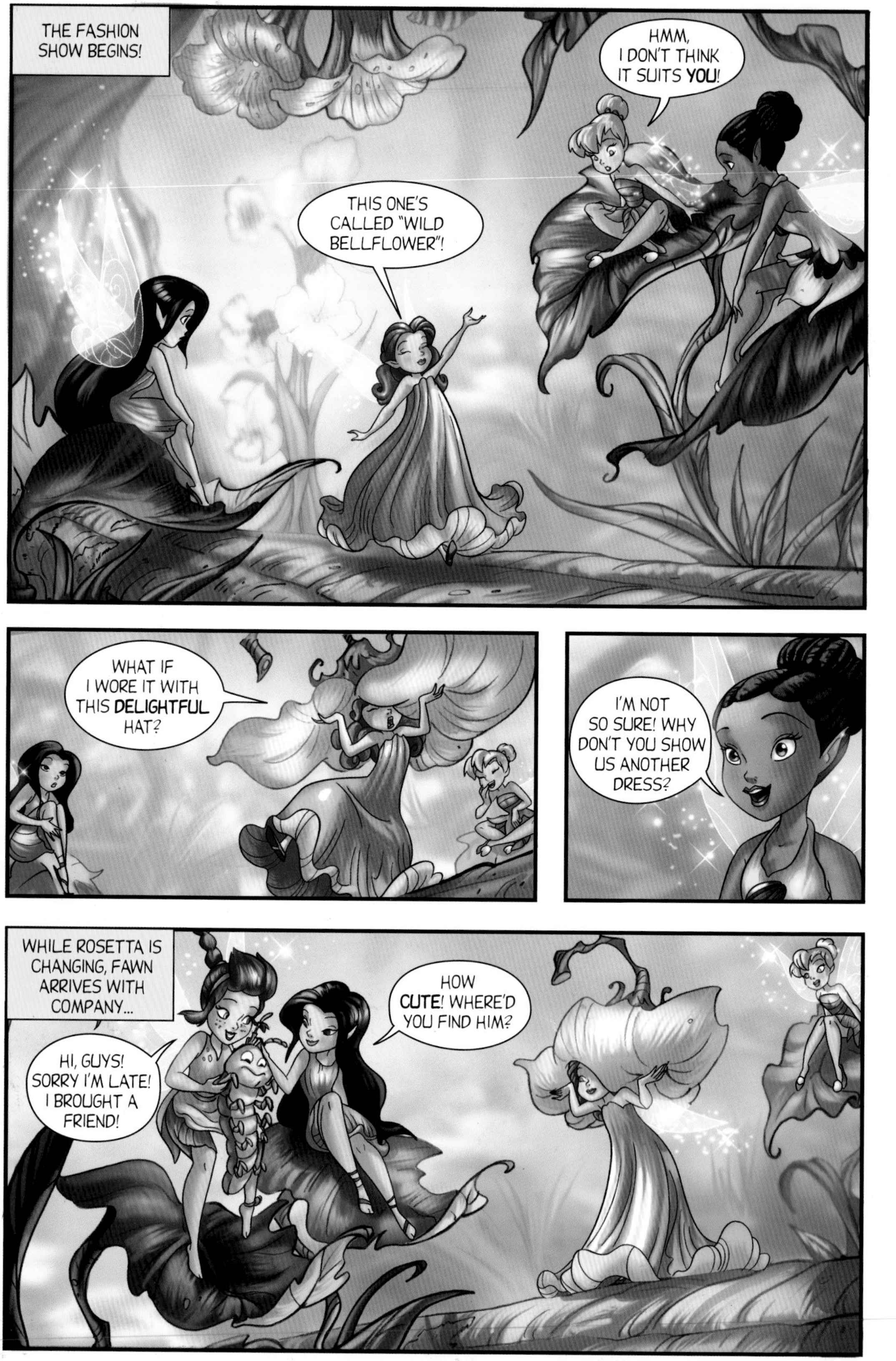
THE FASHION SHOW BEGINS!
HMM, I DON'T THINK IT SUITS **YOU**!
THIS ONE'S CALLED "WILD BELLFLOWER"!
WHAT IF I WORE IT WITH THIS **DELIGHTFUL** HAT?
I'M NOT SO SURE! WHY DON'T YOU SHOW US ANOTHER DRESS?
WHILE ROSETTA IS CHANGING, FAWN ARRIVES WITH COMPANY...
HOW **CUTE**! WHERE'D YOU FIND HIM?
HI, GUYS! SORRY I'M LATE! I BROUGHT A FRIEND!

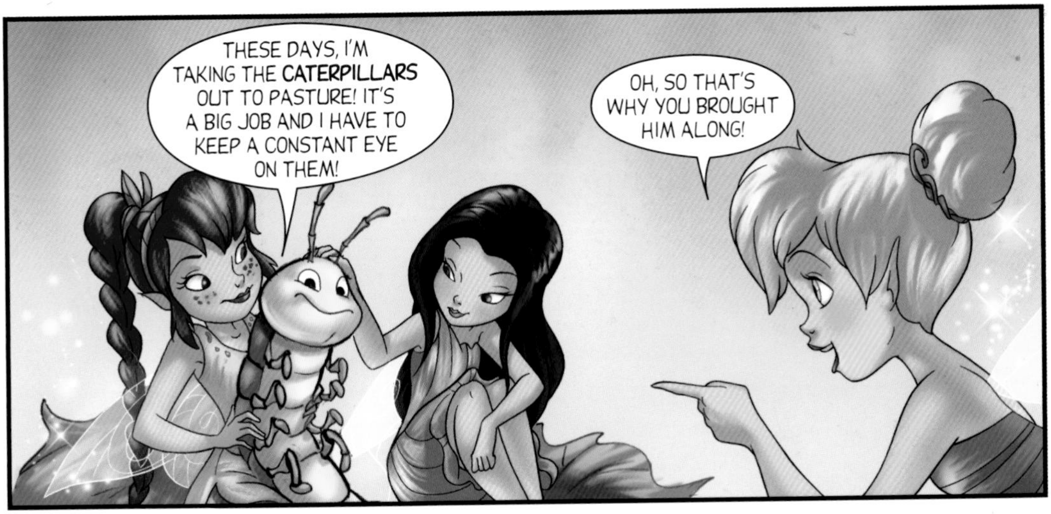
THESE DAYS, I'M TAKING THE **CATERPILLARS** OUT TO PASTURE! IT'S A BIG JOB AND I HAVE TO KEEP A CONSTANT EYE ON THEM!
OH, SO THAT'S WHY YOU BROUGHT HIM ALONG!

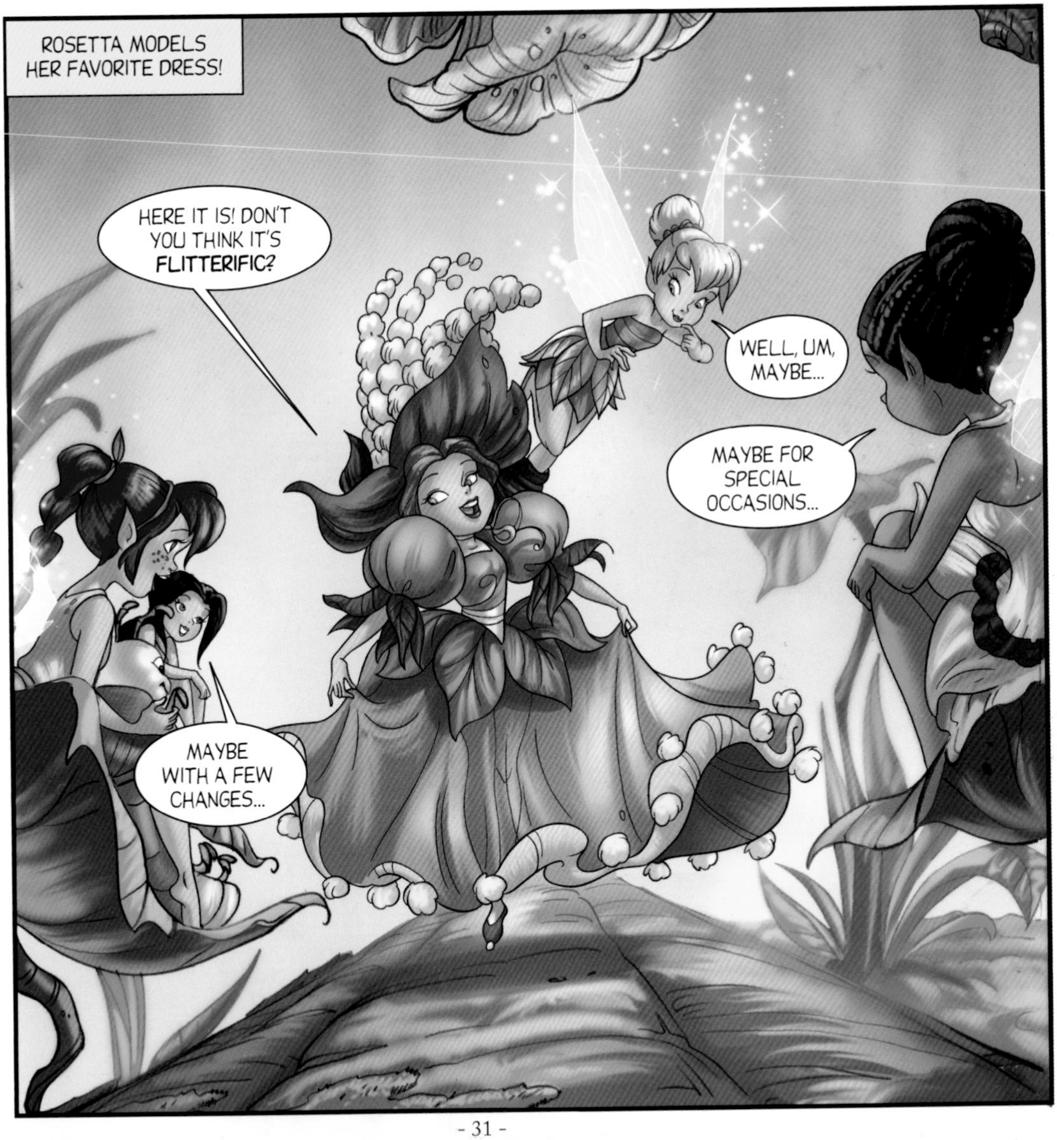
ROSETTA MODELS HER FAVORITE DRESS!
HERE IT IS! DON'T YOU THINK IT'S **FLITTERIFIC?**
WELL, UM, MAYBE...
MAYBE FOR SPECIAL OCCASIONS...
MAYBE WITH A FEW CHANGES...

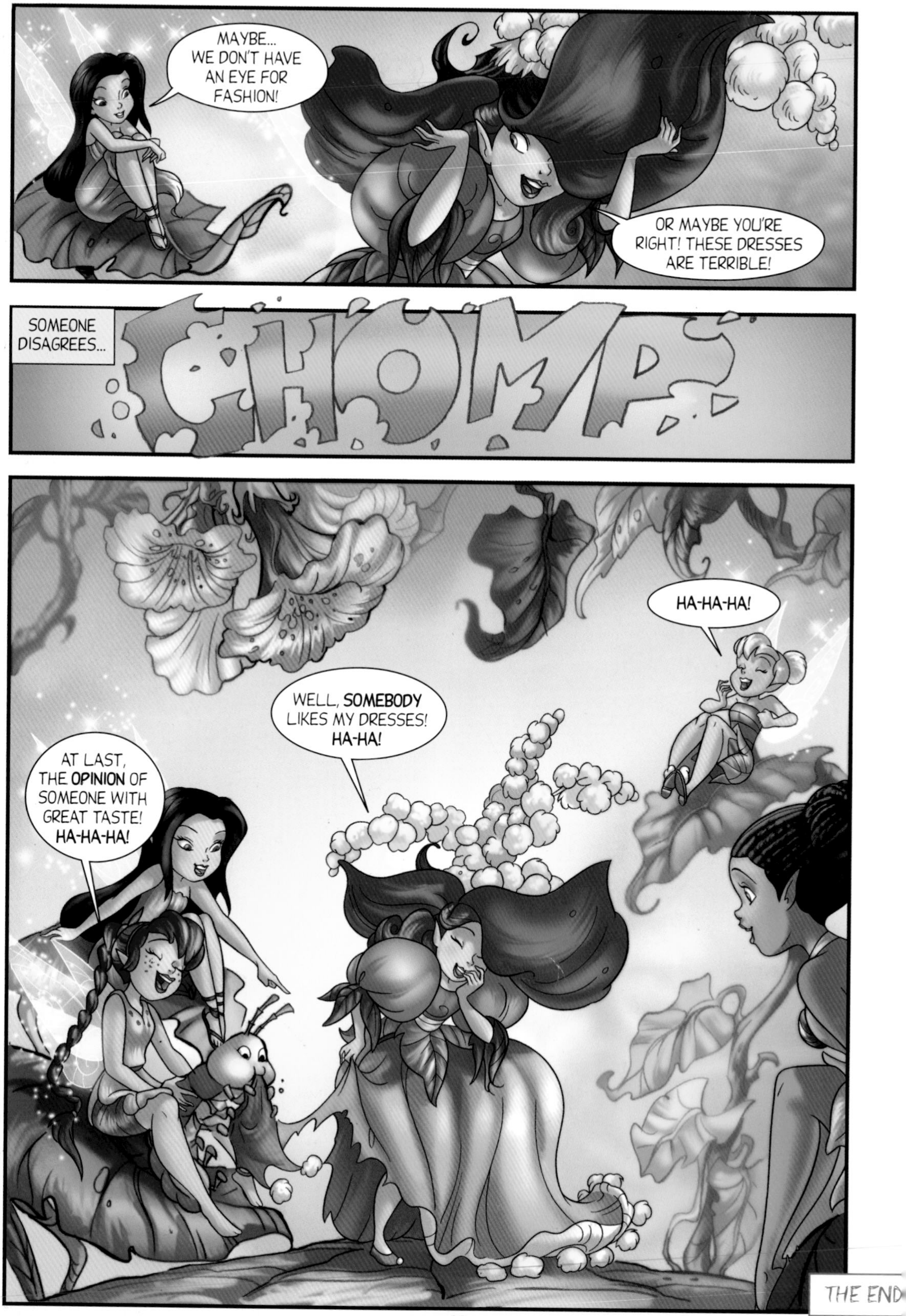
MAYBE... WE DON'T HAVE AN EYE FOR FASHION!
OR MAYBE YOU'RE RIGHT! THESE DRESSES ARE TERRIBLE!
SOMEONE DISAGREES...
CHOMP
HA-HA-HA!
WELL, **SOMEBODY** LIKES MY DRESSES! **HA-HA!**
AT LAST, THE **OPINION** OF SOMEONE WITH GREAT TASTE! **HA-HA-HA!**
THE END

One for All, All for One!

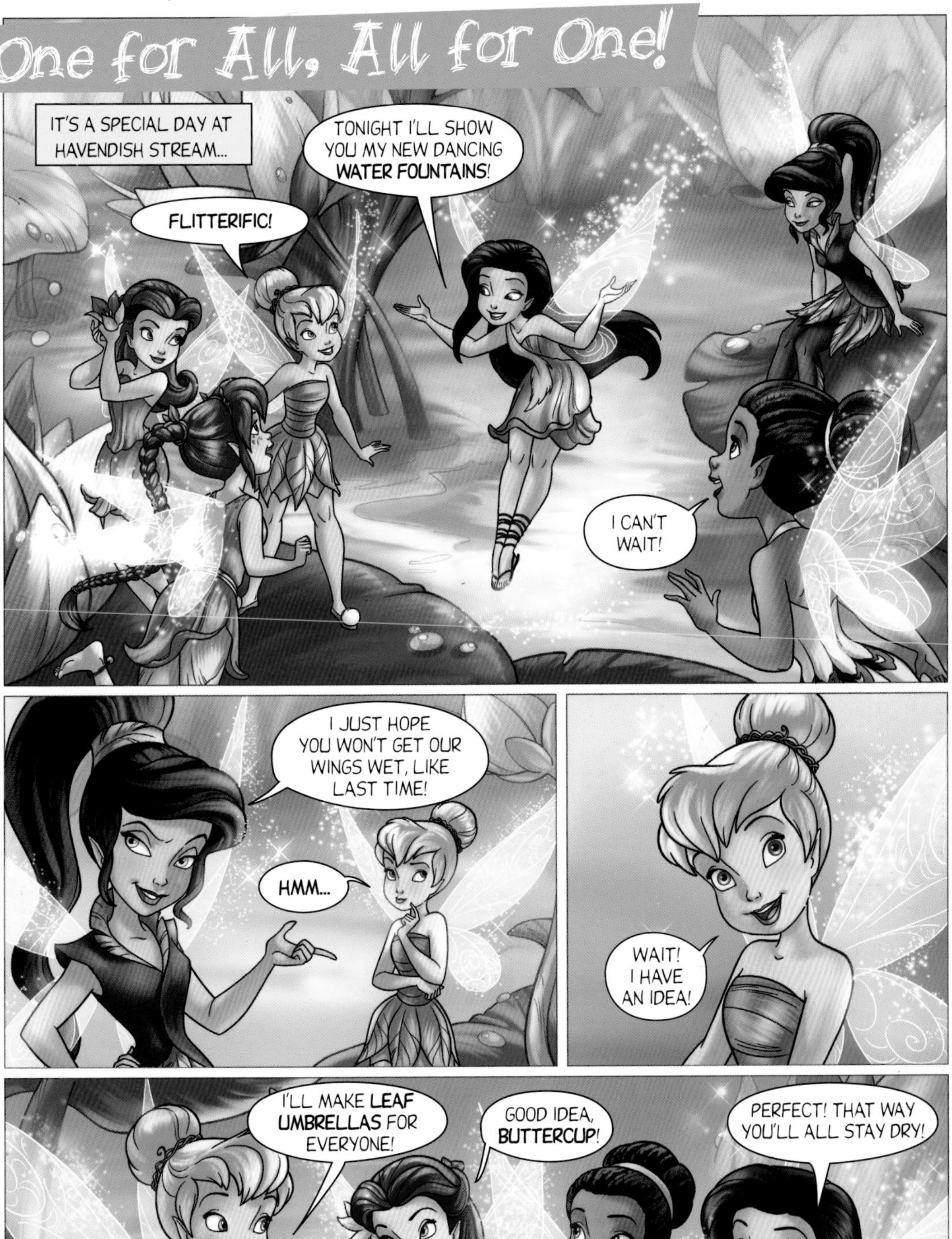

IT'S A SPECIAL DAY AT HAVENDISH STREAM...
TONIGHT I'LL SHOW YOU MY NEW DANCING WATER FOUNTAINS!
FLITTERIFIC!
I CAN'T WAIT!
I JUST HOPE YOU WON'T GET OUR WINGS WET, LIKE LAST TIME!
HMM...
WAIT! I HAVE AN IDEA!
I'LL MAKE LEAF UMBRELLAS FOR EVERYONE!
GOOD IDEA, BUTTERCUP!
PERFECT! THAT WAY YOU'LL ALL STAY DRY!

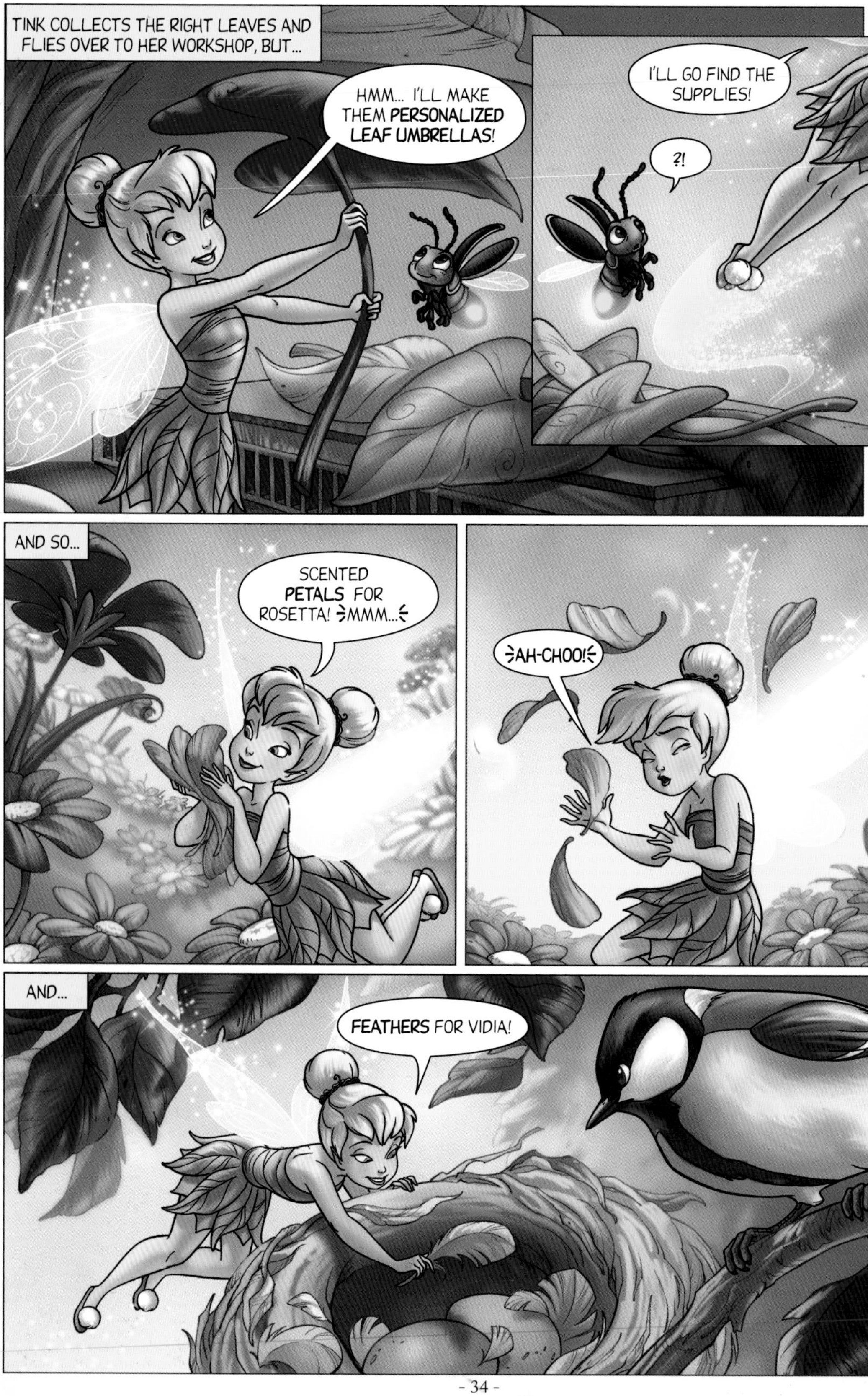
TINK COLLECTS THE RIGHT LEAVES AND FLIES OVER TO HER WORKSHOP, BUT...
HMM... I'LL MAKE THEM **PERSONALIZED LEAF UMBRELLAS**!
I'LL GO FIND THE SUPPLIES!
?!
AND SO...
SCENTED **PETALS** FOR ROSETTA! MMM...
AH-CHOO!
AND...
FEATHERS FOR VIDIA!

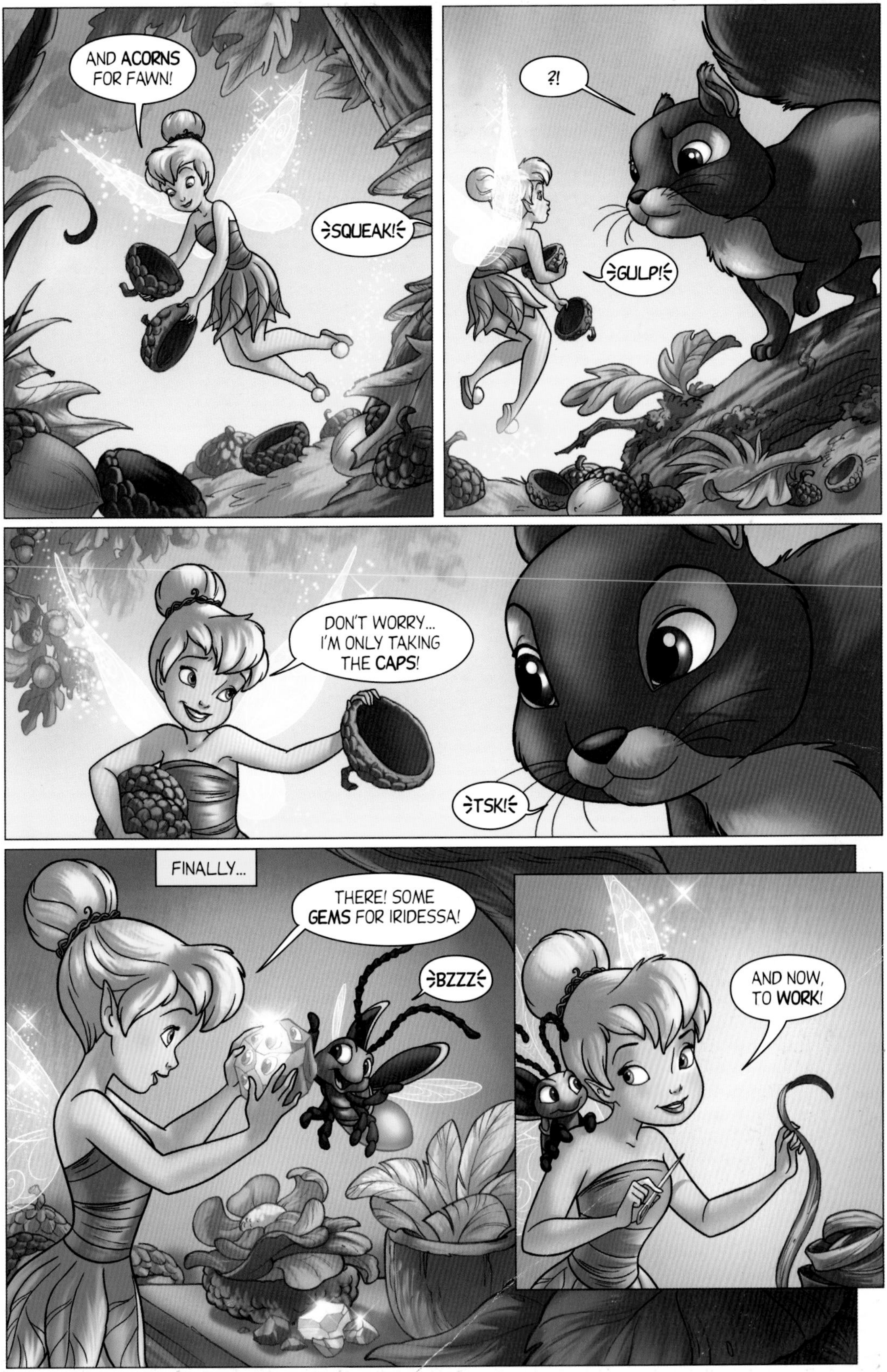
AND ACORNS FOR FAWN!
SQUEAK!
?!
GULP!
DON'T WORRY... I'M ONLY TAKING THE CAPS!
TSK!
FINALLY...
THERE! SOME GEMS FOR IRIDESSA!
BZZZ
AND NOW, TO WORK!

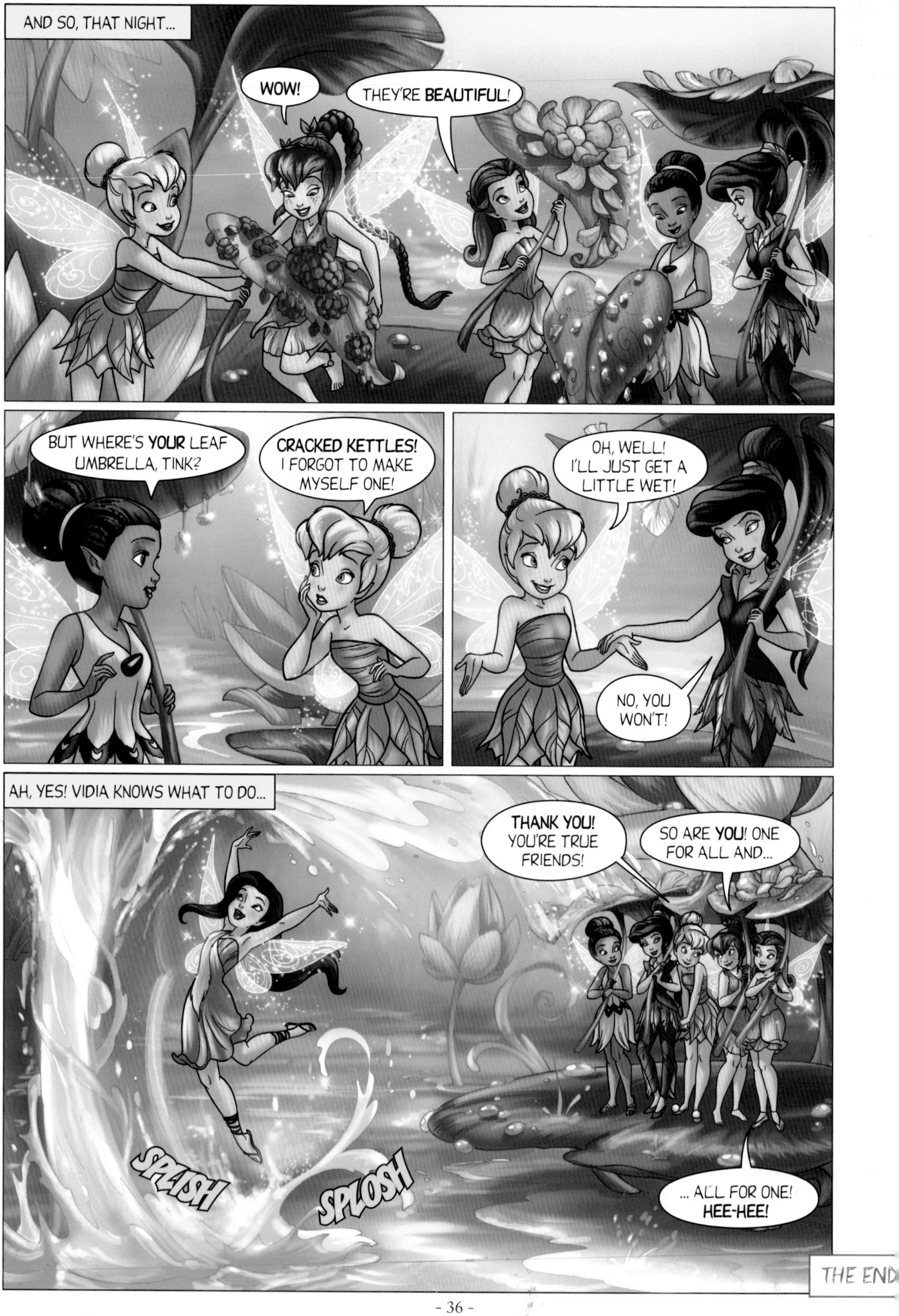
AND SO, THAT NIGHT...
WOW!
THEY'RE **BEAUTIFUL**!
BUT WHERE'S **YOUR** LEAF UMBRELLA, TINK?
CRACKED KETTLES! I FORGOT TO MAKE MYSELF ONE!
OH, WELL! I'LL JUST GET A LITTLE WET!
NO, YOU WON'T!
AH, YES! VIDIA KNOWS WHAT TO DO...
SPLISH
SPLOSH
THANK YOU! YOU'RE TRUE FRIENDS!
SO ARE **YOU**! ONE FOR ALL AND...
... ALL FOR ONE! **HEE-HEE!**
THE END

The Difficult Delivery

IN THE WINTER WOODS, SOMEONE IS MAKING PROGRESS...

WELL DONE, GIRLS!

SWISH

SWISH

CLAP

CLAP

CLAP

WITHOUT YOU, WE NEVER WOULD'VE LEARNED HOW TO ICE SKATE!

YEAH! YOU'RE A FLITTERIFIC TEACHER, GLISS!

HEE-HEE!

HOW CAN WE REPAY YOU?

ARE YOU KIDDING? IT'S BEEN A PLEASURE!

COME ON, MAYBE YOU'D LIKE A PRETTY FLOWER, A JUICY BERRY, OR...?

WELL, IF YOU INSIST...

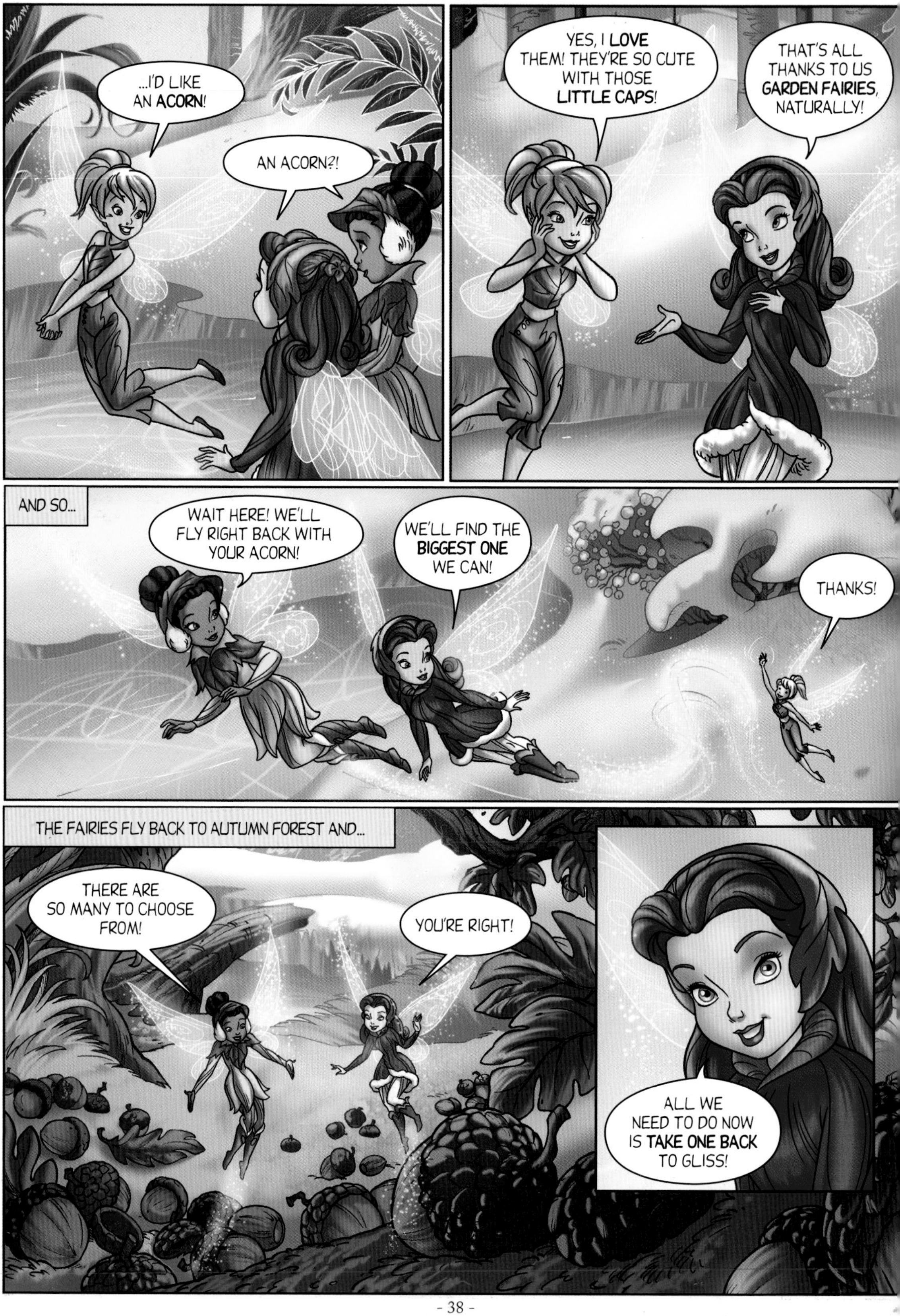
...I'D LIKE AN **ACORN**!
AN ACORN?!
YES, I **LOVE** THEM! THEY'RE SO CUTE WITH THOSE **LITTLE CAPS**!
THAT'S ALL THANKS TO US **GARDEN FAIRIES**, NATURALLY!
AND SO...
WAIT HERE! WE'LL FLY RIGHT BACK WITH YOUR ACORN!
WE'LL FIND THE **BIGGEST ONE** WE CAN!
THANKS!
THE FAIRIES FLY BACK TO AUTUMN FOREST AND...
THERE ARE SO MANY TO CHOOSE FROM!
YOU'RE RIGHT!
ALL WE NEED TO DO NOW IS **TAKE ONE BACK** TO GLISS!

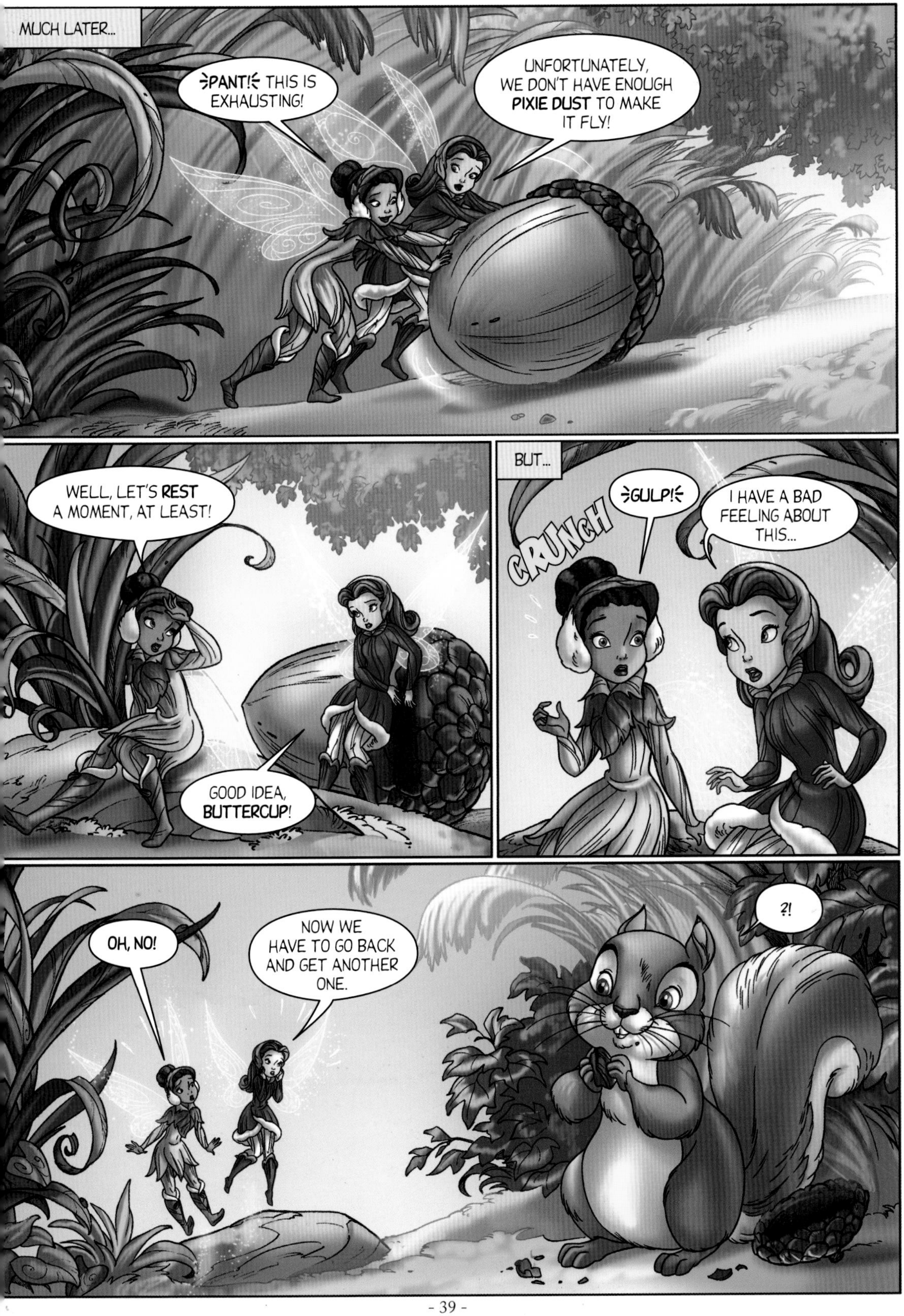
MUCH LATER...
⋟PANT!⋞ THIS IS EXHAUSTING!
UNFORTUNATELY, WE DON'T HAVE ENOUGH PIXIE DUST TO MAKE IT FLY!
WELL, LET'S REST A MOMENT, AT LEAST!
GOOD IDEA, BUTTERCUP!
BUT...
CRUNCH
⋟GULP!⋞
I HAVE A BAD FEELING ABOUT THIS...
OH, NO!
NOW WE HAVE TO GO BACK AND GET ANOTHER ONE.
?!

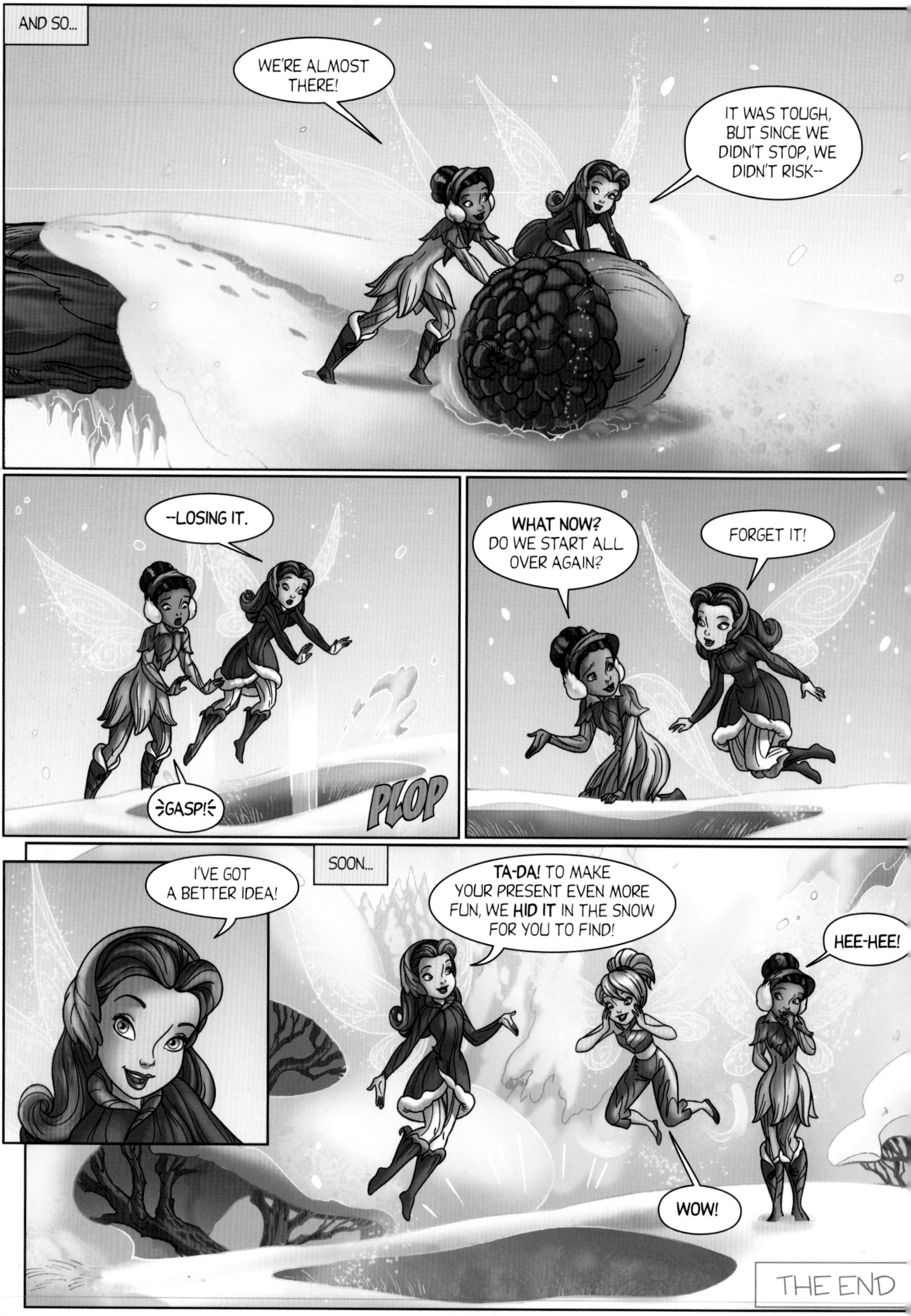
AND SO...
WE'RE ALMOST THERE!
IT WAS TOUGH, BUT SINCE WE DIDN'T STOP, WE DIDN'T RISK--
--LOSING IT.
GASP!
PLOP
WHAT NOW? DO WE START ALL OVER AGAIN?
FORGET IT!
I'VE GOT A BETTER IDEA!
SOON...
TA-DA! TO MAKE YOUR PRESENT EVEN MORE FUN, WE HID IT IN THE SNOW FOR YOU TO FIND!
HEE-HEE!
WOW!
THE END

- 43 -

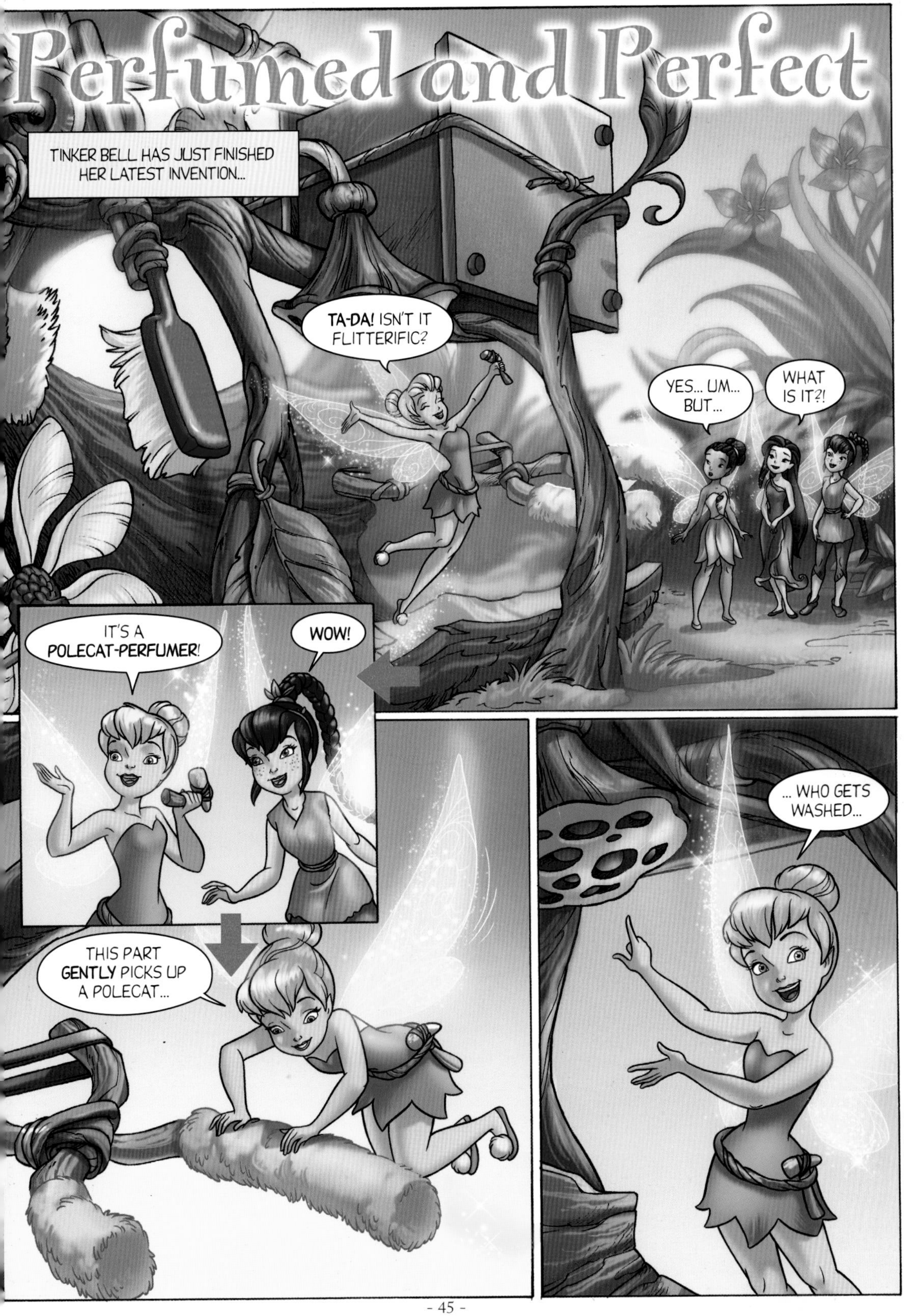

Perfumed and Perfect
TINKER BELL HAS JUST FINISHED HER LATEST INVENTION...
TA-DA! ISN'T IT FLITTERIFIC?
YES... UM... BUT...
WHAT IS IT?!
IT'S A POLECAT-PERFUMER!
WOW!
THIS PART GENTLY PICKS UP A POLECAT...
... WHO GETS WASHED...

Good Night, Bunny!

EACH OF YOU WILL TELL FLUFFY A BEDTIME **STORY**...

TONIGHT FAWN NEEDS HER FRIENDS' HELP...

YOU THINK IT'LL WORK?

SURE! **FLUFFY** LOVES BEDTIME STORIES, THEY HELP HIM FALL ASLEEP!

GREAT! I'VE READ A FEW ON THE MAINLAND!

ME TOO!

BUT FLUFFY HAS NO INTENTION OF SLEEPING JUST YET...

HEY, LITTLE BUNNY! LOOK WHO I'VE BROUGHT FOR A VISIT!

MAKE YOURSELF COMFY AND **LISTEN CAREFULLY!**

?!

ARE YOU READY FOR SOME BEDTIME STORIES?

- 51 -

Cooking Talent?

A Little Nap

ROSETTA IS SHARING WITH HER FRIENDS HER PASSION: HER NATURAL BEAUTY RECIPES...

... MIX HOT WATER WITH CLAY TO GET A BODY MASK THAT WILL CLEANSE AND RELAX YOUR SKIN...

WOW!

CLAY?

CLAY... YOU MEAN MUD?

Rosetta's Beauty Spot

IN ANY CASE, IT'S 100% NATURAL! SO, WHO'S IN?

ME!

ME TOO... I'VE JUST THE THING TO MIX THE BODY MASK!

COME ON... LET'S GO AND GET THE CLAY!

OKAY, WE'LL HELP YOU TOO!

WHILE THE FAIRIES GO OFF TO GET THE INGREDIENTS, BOBBLE HAS DISCOVERED THEIR LITTLE HIDEAWAY...

OOOOOH... WHAT IS THIS PLACE?

≥YAWN!≤ THIS PLACE IS SO RELAXING THAT IT'S MAKING ME FEEL SLEEPY... AND THIS POD SEEMS TO BE MADE JUST FOR ME...

WATCH OUT FOR PAPERCUTZ

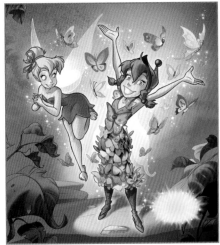

.come to the totally Tinker Bell-filled (Well, except for a couple of stories!) ntieth DISNEY FAIRIES graphic novel from Papercutz—those not-too secretive :s dedicated to publishing great graphic novels for all ages! I'm Jim Salicrup, the :or-in-Chief and honorary member of The Lost Boys, and I'm here to take a few nents to look back and celebrate our twentieth DISNEY FAIRIES graphic novel...

ou were one of the lucky ones who picked up the very first printing of DISNEY RIES #1, you would've seen one of our most embarrassing boo-boos—we identally featured Beck on the front cover instead of Prilla! DISNEY FAIRIES #1 titled "Prilla's Talent," and it did indeed feature a story called "Prilla's Talent," ch was all about that particular fairy's unique talent. What DISNEY FAIRIES #1 not include was a story called "The Most Beautiful Dress," the story that featured fairy called Beck. That story was published in DISNEY FAIRIES #2 "Tinker Bell the Wings of Rani." Oopsie!

fortunately, one of the wonderful things about graphic novel publishing, and ok publishing in general, is that when a book sells out of its print run, if there's enough demand for the book, it'll go back to press, and that provides the portunity for publishers to correct any mistakes that may've slipped by in the vious printings. DISNEY FAIRIES #1 sold out quickly and eventually we replaced original cover of DISNEY FAIRIES #1 with the current cover, which shows Tinker kinda shushing you. Guess she doesn't want anyone to notice that Prilla's still on the cover! Hey, as revealed in DISNEY FAIRIES #1, page 12, panel 1, the fairies call us humans "Clumsies"! I guess now we know y! And if you're wondering exactly what is Prilla's talent, I'm happy to inform you that all twenty DISNEY FAIRIES graphic novels are available at booksellers everywhere, and at all the very best libraries. Another bit of DISNEY FAIRIES lore was also revealed in DISNEY RIES #1—that the fairies never say they're sorry. Instead they say "I'd fly backward if I could." So, at this very late date, I hope you'll w this humble "Clumsy" to offer a sincere "I'd fly backward if I could"!

ile we're talking about the DISNEY FAIRIES graphic novels, here's a quick trivia question to test your knowledge regarding the special ory of this graphic novel series: How many DISNEY FAIRIES graphic novels has Papercutz published? If you answered 20, you're close! But correct answer is 21! In addition to the twenty DISNEY FAIRIES graphic novels in this series, we also published a graphic novel adaptation *Tinker Bell and the Great Fairy Rescue* as a separate title. But that wasn't the only Tinker Bell movie adaptation we published...

NEY FAIRIES #12 featured "Tinker Bell and the Lost Treasure," #13 adapted "Tinker Bell and the Pixie Hollow Games," #15 brought us nker Bell and the Secret of the Wings," #16 included "Tinker Bell and the Pirate Fairy," and finally, #17 told the story of "Tinker Bell the NeverBeast"! Each of these graphic novels make perfect companions to the Tinker Bell Disney DVDs!

Disney
MINNIE
&
DAISY
BEST FRIENDS FOREVER
ASHION
ASSION
PAPERCUTZ

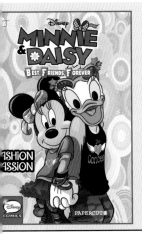

DISNEY FAIRIES was the first DISNEY GRAPHIC NOVEL series published by Papercutz, and we're happy to say we've since added the following Disney series to the Papercutz line-up of great graphic novels:

X-MICKEY – Join Mickey Mouse as he explores all sorts of spooky supernatural mysteries!

DISNEY PARODIES – Imagine great works of literature or the most popular movies of all time spoofed and recast with all your favorite Disney stars! The first volume featured "Mickey's Inferno," a satirical retelling of Dante's *Divine Comedy*! Volume Two kicks into warp drive and spoofs *Star Wars* in "Planetary Wars."

MINNIE & DAISY – Fun-filled High School hi-jinks starring Minnie Mouse and Daisy Duck and their friends. Check out the preview of MINNIE & DAISY #2 "Fashion Passion" on the pages following!

THE ZODIAC LEGACY – An all-new team of super-powered teenagers, created by Stan Lee, the co-creator of *Spider-Man, Iron Man, Thor, Dr. Strange,* and many more!

TAY IN TOUCH!

MAIL:	salicrup@papercutz.com
'EB:	papercutz.com
WITTER:	@papercutzgn
ACEBOOK:	PAPERCUTZGRAPHICNOVELS
EGULAR MAIL:	Papercutz, 160 Broadway, Suite 700, East Wing, New York, NY 10038

And that's not all! Coming soon from Papercutz is an all-new line of graphic novels for girls called Charmz, and one of the graphic novel series included in that line is an all-new series created by Disney! What is it? Check out papercutz.com for the full story! In the meantime, there are plenty of other DISNEY GRAPHIC NOVELS available to keep you busy, so keep on believing in "faith, trust, and pixie dust"!

Thanks, JIM

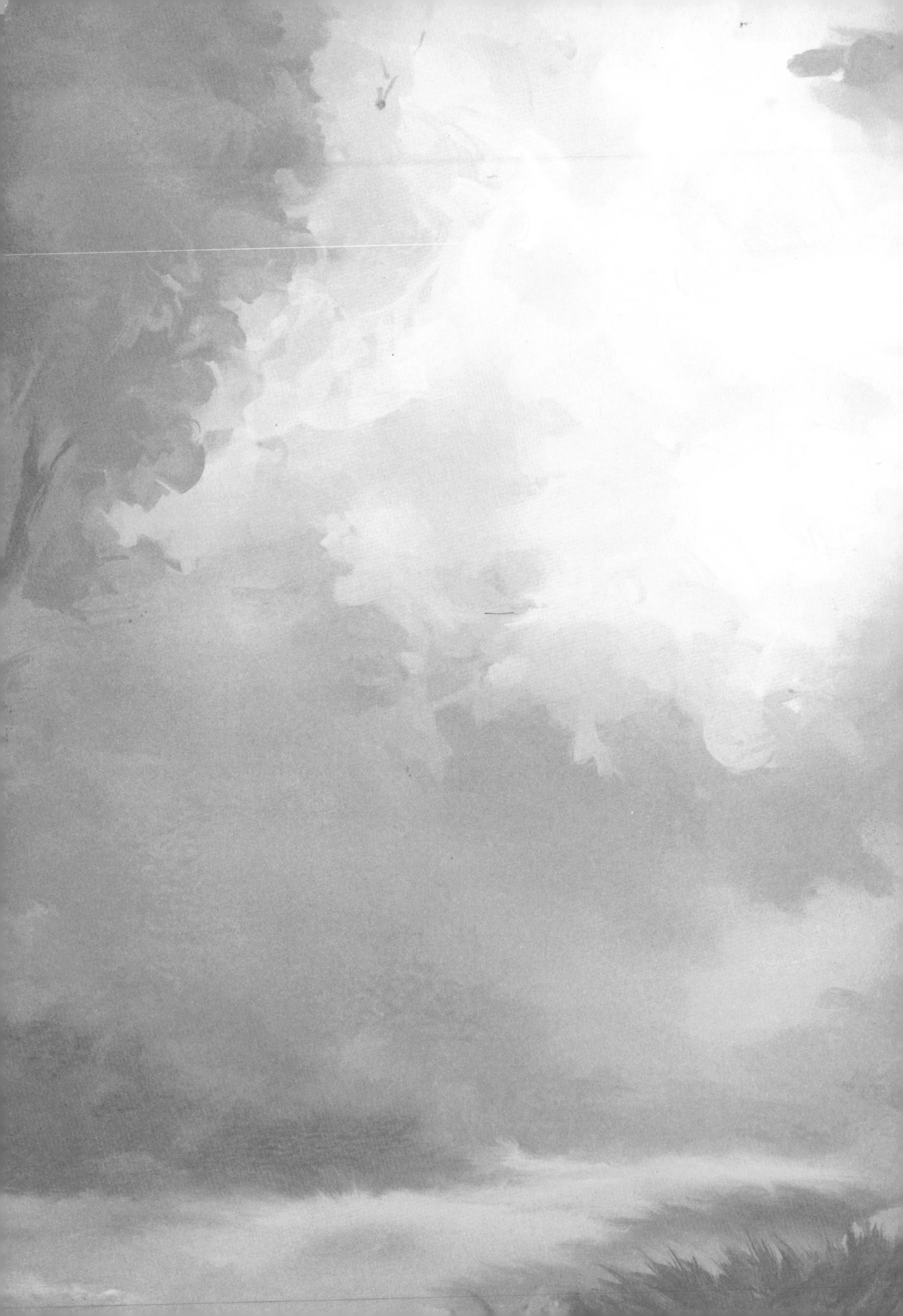